BESTSELLING AUTHORS
IN THE SPOTLIGHT

Dear Reader,

It's time to shine the spotlight on six special authors—bestsellers you wouldn't want to miss!

We've selected stories by some of your favorite authors to give you a chance to meet old friends or discover new ones. These novelists are strong, prolific women who write the stories that you've told us you love, and each is distinguished by a unique style and an uncanny ability to touch the heartstrings of her readers.

If you're not acquainted with the work of Alicia Scott, Sherryl Woods, Barbara Boswell, Kristine Rolofson, Janice Kay Johnson and Muriel Jensen, now's your big chance! And if you are, you may want to have a peek at page six for a more complete listing of books by the author of this volume.

Take a chance on a sure thing, and enjoy all six of our Bestselling Authors in the Spotlight!

The Editors

Praise for the work of
KRISTINE ROLOFSON

**BESTSELLING AUTHORS
IN THE SPOTLIGHT**

KRISTINE ROLOFSON

MADELEINE'S COWBOY

Harlequin Books

TORONTO • NEW YORK • LONDON
AMSTERDAM • PARIS • SYDNEY • HAMBURG
STOCKHOLM • ATHENS • TOKYO • MILAN
MADRID • WARSAW • BUDAPEST • AUCKLAND

ISBN 0-373-83360-1

MADELEINE'S COWBOY

Copyright © 1994 by Kristine Rolofson.

Dear Reader,

Cowboys have always been my heroes.
Madeleine's Cowboy was my first novel to feature
such a man, and what fun it was to write about him!

I learned to love cowboys when my grandfather
handed me his battered copy of Zane Grey's
The Light of the Western Stars. A romantic tale of love,
loyalty, bandits and hidden treasure, it became my
favorite book. I still open the pages and climb into that
world whenever I need to escape.

Like Madeleine, the sight of a man in dusty cowboy
boots leaves me weak-kneed, and I suspect I'm not
alone. When a cowboy takes off his boots, I know he
means business, and readers do, too! The cowboy hero
sweeps the heroine onto his horse, protects her from
danger and, at the same time, gives her an adventure she
will always remember and a love she will never regret.
Now who wouldn't want to ride off into the sunset with
a hero like that? Cowboys and romance go together, like
biscuits and beans, campfires and tall tales, denim and
leather. They always have, and—I hope—they always
will.

I hope you like Madeleine's adventure. I suspect
Zane Grey and my grandfather would have enjoyed
it, too.

With love,

Kristine Rolofson
P.O. Box 323
Peace Dale, RI 02883

A Selection of Kristine Rolofson's Titles

TEMPTATION

#594 BABY BLUES
#607 PLAIN JANE'S MAN
#648 JESSIE'S LAWMAN
#660 MAKE-BELIEVE HONEYMOON
#669 THE COWBOY
#704 THE TEXAN TAKES A WIFE
#717 THE LAST MAN IN MONTANA
#721 THE ONLY MAN IN WYOMING
#725 THE NEXT MAN IN TEXAS
#753 THE BRIDE RODE WEST

HOMETOWN REUNION

#7 A TOUCH OF TEXAS

1

THE NEW MEXICO TRAIN station looked nothing like the building Madeleine Harmon had pictured from the pages of *The Lights of the Desert Stars*. Of course, she reminded herself, the book had been written in 1914. A train station was bound to have changed in seventy-nine years. The stars would still be the same, though. Louis Grey had written so eloquently about them, and tonight she'd see some of those desert stars in person.

She could hardly wait.

Everyone at the station looked as if they knew exactly where they were going and what they would do when they arrived, but no one held a sign for the Ripple K Ranch. No one was searching for a tenderfoot from Connecticut. Still, she supposed someone would be here eventually. She hoped it wouldn't be long. She hated to waste even a few minutes of her vacation, sitting in a crowded train station.

Maddy stood, hoping to see someone with a sign for the ranch. Surely she couldn't be the only person arriving a day early. Three weeks ago she'd called the ranch and explained the situation, and the woman in charge of reservations hadn't seemed concerned, except to warn of a small fee for an extra night's lodging. That was no problem, Madeleine had decided. She didn't have an unlimited vacation budget, but to sleep on a ranch tonight would be worth any price.

Just then she noticed a man enter the large room. He tipped his hat back slightly and surveyed the area. Maddy felt an odd sense of expectation. If this was the cowboy sent to fetch her, he'd been worth the wait. Someone spoke to him, and he nodded and shook hands with the brown-suited older man. Too bad. He certainly looked as if he came from someplace called the Ripple K. Then the cowboy excused himself and continued looking around the room, raising Maddy's hopes once again. He looked impatient and hot, but he didn't carry a sign. Still, Maddy couldn't help hoping this man was the one sent to pick her up. She decided to watch and wait, unwilling to approach a stranger and ask if he was looking for her. Long minutes later, almost as if she'd willed it, the lean, unsmiling cowboy stood in front of her.

"Excuse me, ma'am," he said. Wearing worn denim jeans, dusty boots and a long-sleeved cotton shirt, he was anywhere between thirty and forty. Handsome, lean, unsmiling—perfect, just like the men in the Western novels. Did men really dress that way in New Mexico or was this part of the dude-ranch atmosphere? Real or costume, she loved it.

"Yes?"

"Are you the woman here for the Triple J?"

Maddy hesitated, trying to interpret his Western drawl. "Yes, I suppose I am. I'm—"

"Good," he said, sounding relieved. He stuck out one large brown hand. "Stuart Anderson. Welcome to New Mexico."

He spoke as if she should recognize his name. Maddy didn't want to hurt his feelings, so she smiled and shook his hand. "Thank you. I'm sure I'm going to enjoy myself very much."

He frowned, his handsome face creasing into two vertical lines on either side of his mouth. A hard-looking mouth, Maddy noted, but that was typical of Western men. She looked higher, above a prominent nose, to a pair of startling ice-blue eyes. Dark lashes, dark skin, forehead hidden by the wide-brimmed straw cowboy hat. She assumed his hair was brown, but she couldn't tell unless he removed his hat.

Cowboys didn't remove their hats. Not in public, anyway. She knew that much.

"Your luggage?"

"Over there. I hope I have everything I need." She pointed to the two brand-new duffel bags, hot pink lined with lavender. He picked up the two bags while Maddy stood and hoisted her large, flowered tote over her shoulder. "I wasn't sure what to pack. I've never been out West before."

"Well, you sure are now. It's a long ride to the ranch, so I'll explain everything on the drive. Follow me."

She did, unwilling to lose sight of her luggage or the tall cowboy. He was so serious. Well, she'd read that ranch life made men that way. Still, she hoped that some of the other cowboys would have more personality. It had been a long trip, and she looked forward to being around people and staying in one place for the two weeks she was scheduled at the Ripple K.

The unfamiliar heat hit her the minute they left the station. July in New Mexico felt like the hottest August day in Connecticut. She slipped her sunglasses on, glad she'd invested in a new pair.

The truck he led her to was fairly new, but covered with dust. Mr. Anderson tossed her bags in the back with little concern for the carefully packed contents, while Maddy opened the passenger door and eyed the various leather objects that covered the seat.

"Just a minute," he said, coming up behind her. "I'll move those things out of the way." Moving them out of the way meant shoving them aside, leaving room on the seat for Maddy to climb in. She set her bag on the straw-covered floor and reached for her seat belt.

"I have a few errands to do before we head back," he said. "Won't take long."

Maddy didn't care. She looked out the window at the town and wished she could spend time exploring the stores. There was something special she'd been waiting to purchase. "Is there any place I can buy a hat? I guess I'll need one."

He looked surprised, but then recovered. "Yeah, sure." He guided the truck along the city streets and parked in front of a long section of stores. "I'll be in the bank and the post office. There are a couple of stores here. I'll meet you in McGregor's in ten minutes."

Ten minutes didn't sound like very long, but Maddy figured she could buy an acceptable cowboy hat in that amount of time if that was all she had. Until she walked in and saw the hundreds of hats displayed inside the large store. She enlisted the help of a young saleswoman, gulped when she saw the prices, and tried on a few of the brown felt models.

"You need to be very careful in this sun," the woman cautioned. "Always wear sunscreen and stay indoors during the hottest part of the day. You don't want to ruin that pretty skin of yours."

Maddy smiled. "Thanks. I'll remember that." She chose a light brown hat with a leather thong under the chin, a hat that looked as if it meant business. The kind of hat that would make cattle say, "Here comes someone who knows how to rope me."

Maddy wanted to laugh out loud at the picture she made, standing in the middle of the store wearing a brand-new hat and a flowered cotton sundress. Too bad her new cowboy boots were still packed in one of the duffel bags. They would have added a nice touch.

"You ready?" Stuart Anderson stood inside the door and didn't look as if he wanted to step farther into the store.

"I sure am," she said, tucking the remaining bills into her wallet. "I bought sunscreen and a hat. See?" She held it up for his inspection.

He nodded his approval. "That's a cowboy hat, all right."

"I wanted to fit in."

Stuart Anderson looked up at the hat and then back to Maddy's face. He didn't appear convinced. "If you have everything you need, then we'd better get on our way."

She followed him back to the truck. The cowboy drove quickly and efficiently through the afternoon traffic and soon they were on their way south. He turned the air-conditioning on, adjusted the volume of the music on the radio, and didn't say a word.

Well, she'd read cowboys were like that.

Not very many miles passed before the highway slid into desert country. The nervous knot in Maddy's stomach uncurled, leaving excitement in its wake. She couldn't believe she was finally here. After all those years of reading about the West, she was breathing the air, tasting the dust and looking at the desert. She rummaged through her bag for the camera she'd just bought, and took several snapshots of the scenery. This was the trip of a lifetime and she intended to capture every memorable moment on film.

She glanced over at the man beside her. "This is all very exciting, Mr. Anderson."

He shot her a quizzical look before replying. "Well, that's an interesting way of looking at it."

What was that supposed to mean? "I've read so much about this part of the country. To see it in person is a dream come true."

"It's not like the books," he warned. "We're not going to be ambushed by Geronimo and his Apaches on the way to the ranch."

"It will still be an adventure." She wanted to laugh out loud, just because she was out west, she was free, and her whole life shimmered ahead of her, just like the valley before them. "I haven't had very many adventures."

"You've always been a housekeeper?"

That was an odd way to phrase it, but Maddy didn't correct him. What could it matter what this cowboy thought? "Not always," she said, thinking of her accounting days in Hartford. She'd been very young and very stupid. "But for the past three years, yes."

"What made you come all the way out here?"

"My grandfather." She adjusted her sunglasses, glad the strange man couldn't see the tears that always welled up whenever she thought of Lloyd Harmon. "He and I used to read Louis Grey Westerns."

"Louis Grey? You're kidding!"

"No." she looked over at him. "Why? Haven't you heard of him?"

"Yeah, I've heard of him. I think there's some tourist ranch of his near the Grand Canyon. I've never read any of his books, though."

"You should. He writes about this part of the country."

Stuart Anderson shrugged his impressive shoulders. "Never had the time."

"I brought my favorite," Maddy said. "I'd be glad to let you borrow it, if you like."

He shook his head. "Lady, I *still* don't have the time. And at the Triple J, you won't have time to read much, either."

"I know," she said, but with happiness. She would be too busy learning how to ride a horse, enjoying breakfasts on the mesa and sunsets from the deck of the ranch house. Home-cooked meals and a swimming pool. Trout fishing in the mountain streams and camping overnight in the pine forest in the mountains above the ranch. Yes, the cowboy was correct: she wouldn't have much time to read. Maddy looked out the window at the foothills in the distance. The mountains seemed to be getting closer, which meant that the trip across the valley would be over soon. She held her camera up and took another picture.

Her grandfather had been right to insist on this trip. Even when he was dying, he'd made Maddy promise to use the insurance money and take a vacation. See the country the two of them had only read about for years. Well, she was going to live the dream, like the beer commercial said. You only go around once. And, here she was, at long last "going around."

She took another picture. The scenery was incredible—mesas, ridges, foothills, mountains, deserts. You name it, she was seeing it. Maddy stared out the window and practically purred with excitement.

AT LEAST SHE WAS enthusiastic, Stuart decided. A little young, but that might help with Jenna. He'd thought she'd be older. In fact, from her letters he'd assumed she was practically coming out of retirement to take the job. Not that he could afford to be fussy. She was the only person remotely suitable among the small number of people who had answered his ad. If she could do the work and deal with Jenna, then he didn't care if she was eighteen or one hundred and ten.

What did he know about women, anyway? That's what had gotten him into trouble for years—not knowing enough about women. This particular one was hanging on to her camera and taking pictures as if she was on some sort of sight-seeing trip. Well, he'd let her take all the pictures she wanted, as long as she took care of Jenna and made a decent meal.

She was no beauty, thank God. Brown hair, brown eyes, pale skin, bony and talkative. A little too talkative, but he wouldn't be around much to have to listen to her. And Jenna would appreciate the conversation. He preferred honey blondes, with curves in all the right places, and tall enough that he didn't have to bend over like he was talking to a kid. Connie had been one of those sleek silvery blondes, and he should have known better. He would have saved himself a hell of a lot of trouble if he'd been smarter.

Well, he was pretty damn smart now. Although, he amended, thinking of his headstrong stepdaughter, obviously not smart enough.

"How much longer?" she asked, turning to him with an expectant expression.

"About sixty miles."

"What's the closest town?"

"North of the ranch is Lordsburg, farther east is Deming."

"Are they old cattle towns, too?"

"Yes. Originally railroad towns. Mining towns." He decided he'd better start talking about her duties on the ranch, before she started singing "Home on the Range." "My daughter is anxious to meet you," he began. Well, he thought, there was no harm in the small lie. Jenna had threatened to run away when the "jailer" arrived, but he didn't really believe she'd do it.

"Oh?"

"She, uh, gets a little bored out on the ranch."

"How could anybody be bored on the ranch? The information you sent made it sound like paradise."

"Paradise?" he echoed, trying to remember what he'd written. He hadn't meant to make it sound like anything more than it was: a cattle ranch in New Mexico. "Well, maybe. There are some sunsets that will make you think you've landed in heaven."

"Have you always been a cowboy, Mr. Anderson?"

"Stuart," he corrected. "And, yes, I guess you could say I've been a cowboy, a rancher, for as long as I've needed to be."

"You mean you own the ranch?"

"Yeah. For now." He wondered at the same time how long that statement would be true. If Jenna's grandparents had their way, he wouldn't own so much as a blade of grass or a swaybacked mule.

"For now?" she repeated.

"Well—" he shrugged, sorry he'd let his bitterness spill into the conversation "—times are tough, but we're making it."

"Oh." Maddy didn't know what to say to that. From the prices they charged, she figured the Ripple K had to be "making it" pretty well. But she didn't know anything about ranching, so maybe it had to be a lot more expensive than a tenderfoot from New England could imagine.

"Jenna is eleven," Stuart continued. "Going on fifteen. She's had a difficult time since her mother died. And she spent last year trying to flunk fifth grade."

"Is it possible to flunk fifth grade?"

"Yeah, but she'll squeak by if she makes up her work this summer. I don't think the sixth-grade teacher is real excited about having her in the class next year, but I'm sure hoping the summer will make some changes."

"Why?" She didn't know why he was telling her all of this, but since he seemed anxious to talk, she'd let him. It felt good to be driving along in an air-conditioned truck as the desert rolled beneath them and the foothills came closer. A handsome cowboy was talking to her as if she might know something about kids—which she didn't, but he didn't know that—and she was having a good time. A great time.

"I don't expect miracles," he said. "I'm just doing my best. And that's all I expect from the people who work for me."

"That sounds fair," she replied, and wondered why he looked pleased with her response. He almost smiled.

"You can put a tape in if you want," he offered, and Maddy figured that meant he didn't want to talk anymore. "There's a box of cassettes under the seat."

"Okay." She leaned over and found a plastic bin filled with worn cassettes, but a search through them showed that they were mostly Hank Williams, Charley Pride and George Strait. She preferred Clint Black, Suzy Bogguss and Trisha Yearwood. She pulled her tote closer and rummaged through it until she found the cassettes she'd brought to go with her Walkman cassette player and put a Suzy Bogguss tape in the player on the dashboard.

"Who's that?" he asked, as Suzy started singing her latest hit.

"Suzy Bogguss."

"Never heard of her."

She didn't think that required a comment, but finally, after Suzy finished one song and started another, she had to ask, "Well, what do you think?"

"Nice change," he said.

Well, this guy was a man of few words, Maddy realized. The most he'd said was about his daughter, so at least she knew he knew how to talk.

He was a handsome man, but she preferred men who talked. Still, a man in denim and boots was hard to resist. Even one who didn't clean out his truck. The minutes rolled by as the music filled the silence.

"We're here," he said, interrupting Maddy's thoughts of riding through the desert landscape, looking like an ad for Calvin Klein jeans, while photographing the country so she would never forget her Southwestern vacation.

Sure enough, in the distance she could see a ranch nestled against the foothills. It looked enormous, even from what must be miles away. She looked at her watch. "I didn't know the ranch was this far from town."

"You knew what you were getting into," he muttered. "I told you in the letter that I wouldn't be running into town every day."

He had? He must have meant the brochure, the paragraph that read, "Splendid isolation and breathtaking views." Well, Maddy decided, he was right on both counts. "I wasn't complaining," she stated. He was not only quiet, but touchy, too.

"Good." He turned the truck to the right, onto a smooth dirt road. The ranch dipped out of sight as they wound around the hills. Long minutes later the ranch house appeared, situated on a small bluff facing west. It was long and low, large by Eastern standards. Corrals sprawled around the assorted outbuildings, and several cabins and large barns lay farther away, on the flat area, with the dark mountains behind them. It looked more like a small town than someone's home.

"It's greener than I expected," she said, surprised at the size of the ranch. There didn't seem to be anyone around, though. "Where is everyone?"

"Working." He pulled the truck up near the house and turned the engine off. "There's plenty to do around here. And we're not as isolated as you might think."

"I'm not worried."

He nodded. "You can make a list of groceries and supplies, and I'll see that someone gets them for you. You're welcome to take Jenna into town with you, but don't let her out of your sight when you're there." He opened the truck door and pulled his hat lower to shade his eyes. "And don't ever leave this ranch with Jenna without my permission. You're fired if you do."

"Fired?" she echoed. Something was definitely wrong. She didn't want to make grocery lists or baby-sit a child. "How can you fire a guest? A *paying* guest?"

He hadn't heard her, because he'd stepped out of the truck and moved to the back to unload the suitcases.

"Mr. Anderson," she called, climbing out of the pickup and following him. "I think there's something wrong here."

"You've got that right," he muttered. "There's a hell of a lot wrong here, lady, and the sooner it gets fixed the better off we'll all be."

"No, that's not—"

"Dad!" A young girl ran down the steps from the wide front porch toward the truck. She kicked up dust with every stride. Maddy caught a glimpse of a yellow ponytail, a heart-shaped face and faded jeans as the child came to a stop before them. Her father dropped one of the suitcases and reached out to ruffle her hair, but she ducked away from the affectionate gesture.

"Hello to you, too," he said, retrieving the suitcase. "Have you been watching for us?"

The girl shot a curious glance at Maddy and then turned back to her father. "Is that her?"

"Yes, it certainly is. Mrs. Abernathy, I'd like you to meet Jenna." He prodded the girl. "Jenna?"

"Nice to meet you," the girl mumbled, but she didn't look at all happy. She didn't look at all like her father, either. He was dark, lean and rangy, while the child was fair, with blue eyes and tangled platinum hair that looked as if it hadn't been brushed in three days.

"I'm happy to meet you, too, Jenna, but I'm not—"

"I thought you were gonna be old," the girl interrupted. "I'm glad you're not. Nice hat. You just buy it?"

"Yes, thanks. But I'm not—" Maddy tried again, but something cold and wet touched her hand and she jumped sideways before she realized it was a big black dog.

"Homer, stop!" Jenna giggled. "He just wanted to say hi."

Maddy reached down and petted his large head, trying to avoid the drooling mouth. There was a damp spot near the pocket of her dress already. "Nice dog," she said.

"You like dogs?"

Maddy shrugged. "I don't know. I've never had one."

Father and daughter both looked shocked at that statement, but Stuart motioned to the house. "Come on, I'll show you your room."

Maddy opened her mouth and closed it again. Obviously they had her confused with a Mrs. Abernathy, but she'd rather discuss the problem inside the ranch house, with a glass of something cold to drink, instead of out in the hot sun.

She followed them up the wide steps to the covered porch, then inside to a huge room. The place had that lived-in look; almost *too* lived-in. Clothes were draped over chairs, newspapers lay piled on the floor, and several glasses dotted the assortment of end tables. At the far end of the room, at least thirty feet away, stood a massive stone fireplace. The walls were white plaster, and Navajo rugs in muted shades lay on the maroon tiled floor. Two tan leather couches faced each other, a low table in between. A layer of dust covered everything.

On the left was a dining room, its table large and dark and Spanish in design. It looked very old and very well-used, although its surface was covered with a computer and stacks of paperwork.

"The kitchen's back there," Stuart said, pointing past the dining area. "On the left. Beyond that, in the other wing, are the guest quarters."

Finally, the words *guest quarters*. Relieved, Maddy followed him down the hall, curious to see where she would be spending her two weeks. She'd thought there were separate cabins, but "guest quarters" sounded nice, too. The kitchen was large and bright, but needed a scrubbing. There was no sign of anything being prepared for dinner, which was strange. Maybe there was a separate kitchen-and-dining area for the guests.

After seeing that dining room, she certainly hoped so.

Beyond the kitchen lay an empty swimming pool surrounded by tiles and potted plants. Stuart led her through a door down a wide hall and opened one of the doors to reveal a bright bedroom. French doors led to a veranda that faced the pool. "This is yours. There's another room through there, with a connecting bath, but it's empty. You'll have all the privacy you need."

"Thank you. It's beautiful." She went to the doors and looked out at the building across from the pool, a mirror of the one she was standing in. "What is that?"

"The other wing, where Jenna and I have our rooms." He dropped her suitcases on the floor. "I'll show you everything soon enough."

"*I'll* show Mrs. Abernathy," Jenna offered.

Stuart barely hid his surprise. "All right. Then I'll be—"

Maddy figured this was her chance. "Excuse me, but I'm not Mrs. Abernathy. I'm—"

"What do you prefer to be called, then?" he asked, sounding tired.

"Maddy. Maddy Harmon."

He frowned, then tipped his hat back in a gesture of confusion or great thought, Maddy didn't know which. "No, you're Mrs. Abernathy."

She shook her head. "No, I'm Madeleine Harmon, your latest guest. I know I'm a day early, but I called and talked to the receptionist."

"I don't have a receptionist. And you're the house-keeper."

"No. I'm the guest. And this is a dude ranch."

It was his turn to shake his head. "Not in my life-time, lady."

Jenna sat down on the bed and bounced a couple of times. "What's goin' on?"

"Beats the he—heck out of me," Stuart answered. "I thought I'd picked up the housekeeper. If you're not Mrs. Abernathy, then the poor woman must still be at the train station."

"Oh, no," Maddy said. "I'm so sorry. I thought that you were the person sent to pick me up." She went to her tote bag and started rummaging through it. "I have the brochure right here somewhere."

"This isn't a dude ranch," he repeated.

"I'm catching on," Maddy replied. She hoped he'd recognize sarcasm when he heard it. She looked over at Jenna, who grinned at her. Maddy smiled back.

"There were some calls," Jenna offered, swinging her legs. "Maybe you'd better check the answering ma-chine."

"Good idea," he said, turning to leave the room.

"Mr. Anderson," Maddy said, finally finding the folder and waving it at him. "If you'll take me to the, uh, Ripple K, I'll get out of your way and you can find Mrs. Abernathy."

He stepped forward and took the brochure. "Give me ten minutes," he ordered. "Jenna, fix the lady a cold drink and stick a pizza in the oven."

"I'm sick of pizza," she groaned.

"Just do it." He strode out of the room and down the hall.

Jenna stood, knowing she'd better not argue. "Come on, Miss, uh—"

"Harmon. Call me Maddy."

"Okay. What's it short for?"

"Madeleine."

"I never met anybody named Madeleine before."

"I was named after a heroine in a book. In fact, she was a woman from New York who went out West to see her brother. Actually, she was bored with being a rich beautiful socialite and wanted to do something worthwhile with her life."

"And her name was Madeleine?"

"It sure was. And she arrived at the train station and was met by a cowboy who thought she was someone else."

"Like you and Dad."

Maddy chuckled. "Not quite. The Madeleine in the book was very rich and very beautiful. Famous, too."

"You're not famous?"

"Not at all." Maddy followed the child down the hall to the kitchen and watched as Jenna fixed two large glasses of diet cola.

"Oh. Too bad." She carried the glasses over to the round table and set them on an empty spot. "My mother was famous. She was Miss New Mexico once."

"I'm impressed. That's where you got that gorgeous blond hair?"

"Yes. She died two years ago, but I have pictures of her."

"My mother died when I was thirteen. It's wonderful to have pictures, isn't it?"

Jenna took a large gulp of her drink before she answered. "Sometimes."

STUART SWITCHED OFF the telephone answering machine and wondered what the hell he was going to do now.

Was it a crime to want your child to be happy? He didn't think so, but there were a lot of other people who disagreed. The school principal, for one. She thought Jenna needed a woman's influence, some mothering, even some therapy to deal with the loss of her mother. The therapist thought Jenna needed security. And time. And the grandparents, Connie's folks, thought Jenna needed city lights and city polish and all the things that money could buy. It didn't take a psychiatrist to point out that they wanted to replace the daughter they'd lost, but Stuart figured he wasn't going to let them turn out another spoiled woman. One Connie was enough.

Besides, the child was all he had. And they'd been happy, until Connie died and Jenna started acting up in school. A womanly influence was harder to find than anyone could imagine. There weren't too many women to date, and he didn't have the time. And he didn't want another wife. Hell, he couldn't afford a parakeet after paying off all the bills Connie had rung up, in her boredom and revenge. And the upcoming custody battle wasn't going to get him out of the red any faster.

Well, he'd have to go into the kitchen and figure out what he was going to do with his "guest," the little brown-haired lady with the new hat. He hoped she wouldn't cry or make a big scene. God knew, he'd been through enough of those to last three lifetimes.

He was no good at knowing what to do with

women. And he didn't mind admitting it, either. The truth was, ranchers had no business marrying beauty queens.

Or anyone else, for that matter.

woman. And he didn't mind admitting it, either. The
ride was wasted had no business hurrying her any
place.

Or anyone else for that matter.

2

"WELL," STUART DRAWLED, running his hands through
his thick hair as he reentered the kitchen. "This is a
new one."

He had gorgeous brown hair, Maddy noted, as he removed his hat and hooked it on the back of a kitchen
chair. She and Jenna waited for him to continue.

"I guess we have a bigger problem than I thought."

Jenna placed a glass of ice water in front of him.
"Why? What's the matter now?"

"Mrs. Abernathy left a message that she is not accepting the job, after all. Turns out her daughter had
emergency surgery and our new housekeeper went to
San Diego to take care of her grandchildren. She said
she'd be in touch in a few days, in case anything
changed."

Jenna shrugged. "That's okay. We have Maddy
now."

Maddy shook her head. "I'm sorry, Jenna, but I have
reservations at a dude ranch near here. I'm just a tourist, and I won't be staying here." She turned to Stuart.
"I'm supposed to be at the Ripple K Guest Ranch." She
picked the brochure off the table and pushed it toward
him.

"Not tonight, you won't," Stuart muttered, glancing
at the address beneath a colorful picture of desert cac-

tus. He drank the water until there were only ice cubes remaining in the glass.

Maddy stared at him. Surely she hadn't heard correctly. "Excuse me?"

"I mean," he said, "that the ranch you've chosen for your overpriced vacation is over a hundred miles away. That's a two-hundred-mile round trip I'm not going to make tonight. Besides, I can't leave Jenna alone. It'll be dark before I get back."

"She could come with us." Which was a perfectly reasonable solution.

"I get carsick," the child said. "After thirty miles I start barfing."

"Oh." Stuart Anderson turned his gorgeous gaze on Maddy, and she could feel herself wilting. Why did she have to have a weakness for men in denim and dusty boots? "But what do I do in the meantime?"

"Stay here," he said. It was more an order than a suggestion. "I'll take you out to your guest ranch first thing in the morning."

"All right. Thank you." She wasn't sure if "Thank you" was the correct response to someone who'd confused you with another and took you to his house and refused to take you where you were supposed to be, but she'd always been a polite person. New Mexico cowboys weren't going to change her. "I'll call the ranch and tell them I'll be there tomorrow."

"They're expecting you?"

"Yes."

"Then why didn't they pick you up at the station?"

"I'd like to know that myself," she said, picking up the brochure from the table. "May I use your phone?"

"Sure." He stood and led her out of the kitchen to the dining room. Or office, depending on how you looked at it. He gestured toward the phone. "Help yourself."

It took longer than she'd expected to straighten out the person at the other end of the line. When Maddy returned to the kitchen Stuart stood looking inside the refrigerator. He tossed a head of lettuce on the counter, then turned to her. "Hope you don't mind pizza and salad."

It didn't sound like the authentic Southwestern cuisine she'd had her heart set on, but she hid her disappointment. It was already after five, and her stomach rumbled emptily. "Of course not. Is there anything I can do to help?" He looked so grateful she almost smiled, but she didn't want to hurt his feelings.

"Well, sure," he answered, fumbling for a bottle of salad dressing. "You can help with the salad."

"I'm sure you're wishing I was Mrs. Abernathy," Maddy said, reaching for the lettuce.

"Lady," Stuart answered with a hearty sigh, "you don't know the half of it."

She didn't know why she asked, but she'd never been called shy. "Does this have anything to do with almost flunking fifth grade?"

He half smiled. "Yeah."

She began to remove the plastic wrapping from the lettuce. "Mrs. Abernathy was supposed to do more than just wash the dishes?"

"That's right. Jenna's had a hard time since her mother died, but last year was the worst. It was obvious that we needed help around here. So I advertised for a housekeeper and found—or thought I'd found—Mrs. Abernathy. I was expecting an older woman, someone with maternal instincts," Stuart admitted. "You were quite a surprise this afternoon."

"Yes, well, *you* weren't." Stuart Anderson still looked like the perfect cowboy.

He turned the oven on and slid a frozen pizza from its box. "Jenna needs a woman around. *I* need someone to take over this house. I thought I'd fixed both problems at once."

"With Mrs. Abernathy."

"Yeah."

"What about the other people who work on this ranch?"

"The kind of cowboys you're looking forward to meeting at the—what is it?—the Ripple K?"

"Yes."

"I've got a couple of newlyweds in the old cabin in the northwest corner of the ranch. Tom and Cindy Peters." He put the pizza on a cookie sheet and slid it into the oven. "Then there's Mac. He's retired, but he helps me out as much as he can. Five full-time hands, and two youngsters, Billy and Joel. College kids. They live in the bunkhouse."

"What do they do for meals?"

"They pretty much take care of themselves. The bunkhouse is set up with a kitchen."

"Oh." The vision of grizzled cowboys eating chili around a wide-planked table disappeared.

Jenna came back into the kitchen with a box. "This was the last one in the freezer," she said, setting a frozen apple pie on the counter. "We'll have to get more."

"All right."

"And we're out of French fries."

Maddy figured they must live on frozen food seven days a week and felt sorry for them, and then firmly reminded herself that she barely knew these two people and, after tomorrow, would never set eyes on them again. She rinsed the lettuce and shook the excess water from its leaves before pulling it apart with her fingers. Jenna handed her a heavy pottery bowl.

"That's beautiful," Maddy said, carefully taking the bowl and putting it close to the sink.

"We used to collect it," she said. Maddy wondered who "we" was. She assumed Jenna meant her mother, the former Miss New Mexico. "Too bad we don't have the pool ready," Jenna said. "Dad promised as soon as I had someone here to watch me, he'd get it filled and cleaned up."

"Mrs. Abernathy again," Maddy said. "Was she a good cook and a good swimmer, too?"

"Yes," Stuart answered, opening a drawer and removing the appropriate silverware. "Or so she said."

"She sounded like an old bag," Jenna said. "I'm glad she didn't come."

"Jenna, watch your mouth."

Maddy turned so Jenna wouldn't see her smile. This was so different from her life the past three years. Three years caring for an old man suffering from a stroke hadn't put her in contact with children or cowboys. And no frozen meals, either; she'd made every single meal from scratch, which was the way her grandfather preferred it.

"Where did you come from?" Jenna asked.

"Connecticut."

"That's a long way from here. Why'd you come here?"

"For a vacation," Maddy answered, shredding the lettuce with neat motions. "I wanted to learn to ride a horse, and I wanted to see the desert and the mountains and all sorts of places I'd never seen before."

"That's pretty cool," the child said, standing close. "Are you married?"

"No."

"Have a boyfriend?"

"No."

"What do you do in Connecticut?"

"I used to be an accountant," Maddy replied. She didn't mind the child's questions, but Stuart shot her an apologetic look.

"There aren't any secrets around Jenna," he explained. "She knows everything that goes on around the ranch."

"That's okay. I don't mind." Maddy finished the lettuce and watched Stuart slice fat red tomatoes and dump them into the bowl.

"Did you find out what happened with your dude ranch?"

"Not really," Maddy answered, remembering the woman's confusion. "I think they assumed I was driving myself there, especially since I was arriving a day early. It's not really important now."

"You could stay here this summer," the child said. "You could be the housekeeper and I could teach you how to ride." She turned to her father. "Snake would be a great horse for Maddy to ride, wouldn't he?"

Maddy shook her head. "No, thanks, Jenna. I have my plans all made for the summer. New Mexico is just the first stop. I'm going to see Arizona and Nevada, too."

The child looked disappointed. "You sure?"

"Yes," Maddy nodded. "Absolutely sure." She never wanted to cook again. She didn't want to roll one more biscuit or bone another chicken or slice peaches for homemade pie. She didn't want to whip the cream or wipe the dishes.

She was finished taking care of people. She felt as if she'd done nothing else for all of her adult life, and most of her childhood, too. First her father, then her grandfather. Not to mention Richard. Now, there was a topic to be avoided.

"Want a beer?" Stuart asked.

She never drank beer, so she said, "Sure."

He took two icy dark bottles from the refrigerator and opened them with a quick twist of his thumb. He handed her one. "Want a glass?"

"No," she said, watching him tilt the bottle to his lips. "I'll drink it like this." The cold bitter liquid tasted great. It was fun being selfish, Maddy decided. She was going to work at it. She wanted to be one of those women who ate in restaurants every single day. Who had their nails done and their hair highlighted and went out to lunch and to movies starring Kevin Costner. And shopped for shoes they didn't need. Of course, she didn't know anyone like that personally, but she thought she'd like that kind of life-style.

At least for a while, until she decided what she was going to do for the rest of her life.

Stuart grabbed a bag of tortilla chips from the top of the refrigerator. "Appetizers," he explained, pointing to a jar of red sauce on the counter. "Help yourself."

Maddy took a couple of triangle chips and dipped one corner into the sauce. "Is this hot?"

"No."

She watched him take a huge bite of the chip and swallow easily before she took a bite of hers. White-hot sensation filled her mouth and she swallowed quickly before she embarrassed herself and spat it out. Then she took a large gulp of the beer to wash it down. "I think," she gasped, "that was hot."

Jenna shook her head. "I'll bet no one in Connecticut eats salsa."

"Sure, they do," Maddy managed to say. "It's just not on fire when they do."

Stuart almost smiled again. "Sorry. Go sit down at the table and make yourself comfortable. I'll bring the pizza over in a few minutes."

Maddy did as she was told, sitting next to Jenna at the round pine table. She surveyed the kitchen as she sipped from the bottle of beer. It needed to be cleaned, of course. And the view would be wonderful if the pool actually held water.

There was something about the house that tore at her heartstrings. Unloved. That was it. The house needed love and attention, and so did its two occupants. They were like two lost souls, struggling to shred lettuce and heat pizza and deal with the day-to-day chores. Maddy braced herself. In two minutes she'd be filling a bucket with soapy water and starting to scrub the tiled floor.

Worse, she'd figure she was having a good time.

Maddy took another swallow of her beer, growing accustomed to the taste and liking the way it uncurled a knot in her stomach she didn't know had existed. Vacations were supposed to uncurl all those nasty knots, and she'd started hers, even if she was on the wrong ranch. "Have you ever had a housekeeper before?"

Jenna grabbed a chip. "Just Mac."

"The cowboy who lives in the bunkhouse?"

"He has his own cabin, even though I tried to get him to move into the house. Said he was too old to change," Stuart explained. "But his hip bothers him a lot, and he's getting too old for taking care of the house."

"Everyone thinks I need a mother," Jenna grumbled. "But I liked the way Mac cooked."

"The psychologist over at the school thinks having a woman around here would be good for you." Stuart brought the pizza over to the table and set it on a hot pad so the pan wouldn't scar the tabletop. "Better than a couple of beat-up cowboys."

"She thinks she knows everything," Jenna said, rolling her eyes at Maddy. "But she doesn't."

Stuart shrugged. "She knows more about girls than I do."

Maddy didn't doubt that, but she clamped her lips shut to keep from voicing an opinion. If ever there was a child who needed a woman's care, it was Jenna Anderson. Obviously, Miss New Mexico had left quite a void when she died.

"Besides," Stuart continued, "Mac is half blind, partially deaf, and doesn't need to spend his time worrying over grocery lists and whether the rug needs vacuuming. He deserves to spend his time fishing and relaxing."

"He's sick of fishing," Jenna argued.

"Well, I wouldn't be," Stuart said, slicing the pizza into large pieces. "You fish, Miss Harmon?"

"Not yet. And call me Maddy." She lifted her plate and watched as he dumped a quarter of the pizza on it. "Learning to fish is one of those adventures I'm going to be having this summer."

"You have to *learn* how to fish?"

Stuart took Jenna's plate and filled it. "Yes, smartie. It's a skill."

Jenna didn't look convinced. "I thought you just *went*."

"And how many fish have you caught?"

"Two," the child said.

"That's my point," said her father. "You have a lot to learn."

"I can't wait," Maddy said. "We're going on a camping trip up in the mountains and we're going to fish the streams and cook over an open fire and—"

"Sing cowboy songs?"

"Maybe," she said, refusing to be teased. "It all sounds heavenly."

"The mountains are beautiful," Stuart agreed. "And there's nothing like sleeping under the stars."

"That's the way Louis Grey felt, too."

Jenna looked interested. "Who's Louis Grey?"

"An author whose books Maddy likes to read."

"Oh. Boy or girl?"

"Boy. He wrote that book I was telling you about, the one where the rich woman goes to New Mexico to see her brother and is met at the train station by a cowboy who doesn't know who she is."

"Like what happened to you."

Maddy smiled. "I'm not a rich debutante."

"You'd have to be pretty well-off to afford two weeks at one of those dude ranches."

Maddy turned to Stuart. "I'm not, though. My grandfather left me a little money, enough to take a vacation and see the West." More to the point, she wanted to have adventures and see the world. Or at least part of it.

The simple dinner tasted surprisingly good, despite the slightly cardboard texture of the pizza crust. Maddy figured if she stayed away from the salsa her mouth would survive the meal in pretty good condition. Stuart placed another bottle of beer in front of her and she drank that one, too.

Stuart turned to his daughter. "You fed Homer yet?"

"No," Jenna admitted. "I forgot."

"Better do it," Stuart said, gesturing toward the window where Homer waited patiently near the steps to the pool. "He looks ready for dinner."

Jenna didn't look pleased, but she got up and opened a cupboard, then carried a coffee can full of dry dog food outside.

"I put the pie in the oven but it takes an hour or so to bake," Stuart said, standing to clear the plates from the table. Maddy stood, too, and started to help. No one told her to sit down so she carried the plates and silverware to the counter and set them there.

"I hope you're not going to any trouble," she said. "After all, you weren't expecting company."

"I wanted to impress Mrs. Abernathy," Stuart admitted. "I'd hoped she and Jenna would take to each other right away. Do you drink coffee?"

"Yes."

He filled the coffeepot and plugged it in.

"How long have you been a rancher?" It seemed a good time for small talk.

"All my life. This was my father's place, and my grandfather's. I've managed to hold on to most of the ranch. Parts of this house are the original hacienda."

Jenna came back into the kitchen and wiped her hands on her shorts. "Homer's happy."

"Good." He looked at his watch. "If you'll excuse me, I have to check on Mac." He turned to his daughter. "Take the pie out of the oven when the buzzer goes off."

"I *know*," she said. "I do it *all the time*."

"Right," he said, and looked back at Maddy. "Help yourself to anything you want. Coffee should be ready in a few minutes."

"Thanks."

He nodded, grabbed his hat and plopped it on his head. The click of his boots on the tile floor echoed through the house, then she heard the door open and shut.

"Well, that's that," Jenna said. "As usual."

"Your father works hard," Maddy said, feeling as if she had to say something.

"Yeah. That's all he ever wants to do." Jenna tossed the dirty plates in the garbage can. "And he's not my father."

"He's not?"

She shook her head. "He's my stepfather. I was two when my mother married him. So we're not really related."

"Oh," Maddy said, eyeing the filling coffee carafe. She really didn't want to know anything more about this strange household.

"That's why he needs a housekeeper—to take care of me so he won't have to."

"It doesn't sound that way to me," Maddy protested finally. "It seems like he just wants to make sure you're taken care of properly."

The child shrugged. "Maybe. Are you *sure* you don't want to be a housekeeper?"

"Positive," Maddy said. "Absolutely positive." She'd never meant anything more. For now, she was going to see the West. Ride horses. Breathe mountain air and breathe desert air. And, when the summer was over, she'd have her nails done and her hair highlighted and she'd start looking for a job.

And that job wouldn't be keeping house for *anyone*, not even if he was the handsomest man she'd ever laid eyes on.

She wished she hadn't agreed to coffee, wished she could go to bed early instead. All of a sudden the exhausting train trip had caught up with her. Or maybe it was the two beers. Or the long ride in Stuart's old truck.

Whatever it was, Maddy longed for the privacy of "her" room, with its cozy bed. But she couldn't leave Jenna alone in the kitchen. That wouldn't be the best thing for an uninvited guest to do. So the two of them cleaned up, which took about three minutes, and then Jenna sat down at the kitchen table and picked up a paperback book. On the cover a knife dripped bright red blood.

"I think I'll take a shower," Maddy said.

"Do whatever you want."

"What about the pie?"

Jenna looked up from the book. "What about it?"

"You'll take it out of the oven?"

"Sure." She shrugged, stretching her feet to rest on the seat of another kitchen chair. "Don't worry about a thing."

Easier said than done. She wasn't used to children fending for themselves in the kitchen, but then, nothing about this strange household was any of her business.

She made her way down the hall to her bedroom. A layer of dust coated everything, but the room still looked good. She unzipped one of her bags and rummaged through it for a nightgown. The flowered bag with her makeup and toiletries was in her large tote bag, and she took it into the bathroom. The fixtures were white, the walls ivory above the familiar red tiled floor. Bright blue towels hung from rods beside the sink. A large mirror showed Maddy the dark circles under her eyes and the coating of dust on her hair.

A long hot shower solved the dust problem, but the smell of apple pie was too irresistible to be ignored. So instead of a nightgown, Maddy put on her jeans and a blue cotton T-shirt and wandered barefoot toward the kitchen. The buzzer went off as she stepped into the room. Jenna grabbed the pot holders.

"I'll do that," Maddy offered, reaching to the stove to turn off the buzzer.

"Okay." Jenna handed her the blue-checked pot holders and stepped back. "It smells like it's done."

"It sure does." She bent over and opened the oven door. The pie was golden, with bubbling juice spilling over the crust and down the sides of the pan. Stuart hadn't put a pan underneath to catch the drips, so apple juice had splattered and burned on the bottom of the oven. The oven floor looked as if seventy or eighty pies had dripped on it since the last time it had been cleaned.

These people needed help. Maddy closed her eyes briefly, reminding herself that she had last cleaned an oven exactly one week ago. Then she pulled the pie out and set it on top of the stove. "It looks wonderful."

"It's Mac's favorite," Jenna offered. "Dad didn't want him baking anymore so he bought a case of them."

"Mrs. Abernathy!" a grizzled voice called.

Maddy turned around to see an old man entering the kitchen. He was short, bowlegged, with a round face and blue eyes surrounded by weather-beaten, lined skin. "I'm not—"

"She's not Mrs. Abernathy," Jenna interrupted. "Didn't Dad tell you?"

"Then who is she?"

"I'm—"

"Maddy Harmon," the child said, waving toward Maddy. "She's supposed to be on a dude ranch but Dad picked her up by mistake."

"By mistake, huh?" The man looked at her as if she were a fortune hunter, ready to rob the Triple J of all its assets.

Maddy stuck out her hand. "You must be Mac. I'm glad to meet you."

He frowned, shook her hand with his gnarled one, then sat down at the table. "Pie smells good."

"It's the last one," Jenna explained. "Dad's gonna hafta buy more. Mrs. Abernathy couldn't come cuz her daughter's in the hospital somewhere."

Mac chuckled. "Stuart's having a hell of a time replacing me, isn't he!"

"I'm not replacing you," Stuart said, entering the kitchen. "You act as if I'm turning you off the ranch."

Mac ignored him and pointed to the coffeepot. "Pour me a cup of that, will you, Jenna. I've had a mighty long afternoon, and it ain't sundown yet."

Jenna obeyed him, obviously used to taking Mac's orders. Maddy liked him. The twinkle in his eyes belied the gruff exterior. Just like the book, here was the old cowboy, the heroine's adviser and foreman. Maddy shivered. This was starting to get spooky.

"I'm not replacing you," Stuart repeated, pouring himself a cup of coffee. "I'm adding more help around the house."

"Ha," Mac muttered as Jenna set the coffee cup on the table in front of him. "Thanks, honey. You're a good girl."

"That's not what the psychologist says." Jenna grinned.

"That's a load of bullsh—"

"Mac," Stuart warned, then looked over at Maddy. "Have a seat. I'll serve the pie."

"It's hot," Maddy cautioned. "We just took it out of the oven."

"No problem," he said, moving the pie to the center of the kitchen table. "We put ice cream on it."

Within minutes he and Jenna served pie and ice cream, refilled coffee cups and tossed a basket of paper napkins back on the round table. Almost like a real family, Maddy thought, taking a cautious bite of the pie. The ice cream had rapidly turned to cream and dripped between the tines of her fork. The conversation ran to cattle, the weather and how the "college boys" were working out so far this summer. Mac was more optimistic about "the boys" than Stuart was. Authentic ranch conversation, Maddy noted, pleased to have a chance to eavesdrop.

"So," Mac said, turning to Maddy. "You're headed to a dude ranch?"

"Yes. I can't wait." She leaned over to the counter where the brochure lay. "Here," she said, handing it to the old rancher. "It's an authentic cattle ranch."

"Authentic," the man repeated, unfolding the brochure. "Let me see that."

Jenna edged closer. "I told her I could teach her to ride."

"Who?"

"Maddy. If she stayed here. Instead of Mrs. Abernathy." She glanced at Maddy and grinned. "Instead of some old dude ranch. We have everything they have, if Dad would fill the pool."

"Jenna," her father cautioned. "Don't start."

"Now, son, the girl might have a good idea." Mac turned his piercing gaze on Maddy. "You cook?"

Maddy put her fork down, finishing the final bite of her pie. "Yes, I do. But I'm on vacation."

"For how long?"

"The entire summer."

Mac shook his head. "We don't need a housekeeper anyway," he muttered. "Plain foolish, if you ask me."

Stuart stood and reached for the coffeepot. "I didn't ask you."

Mac winked at Jenna. "The last thing we need around this ranch is more women. They're jest trouble and we manage without them jest fine."

Maddy wiped her mouth with her napkin, glad they couldn't see her smile. The people at the Triple J didn't look as if they were managing very well at all, but that was none of her concern. She'd drink her coffee and go to bed and dream about riding the range of the Ripple K tomorrow.

"IT IS TOO A GOOD idea."

"We don't even know the woman."

"We didn't know Mrs. Abernathy, either."

Stuart had nothing to say to that. He found it difficult to argue with Jenna. She came up with the damnedest things. "Forget it, Jen," he said, wishing she was still four years old and liked being tucked into bed. Instead she stood in her doorway, the sound of rap music filling the bedroom behind her. "Miss Harmon," he began, "is—"

"Maddy," Jenna corrected.

Stuart ignored her. "Is leaving tomorrow morning," he finished. "Maybe the Abernathy woman will be able to come here sooner than we think."

"I am going to have a *lousy* summer," Jenna moaned. "No pool, no friends, just an old lady who knows how to swim. At least Maddy is *young* and wouldn't *embarrass* me."

"Good night, honey," Stuart said, hoping Jenna would hold out her arms for a hug. Instead she sighed and turned away.

"Night, Dad." The door shut.

Stuart stood in the hall for a long moment before heading toward his own bedroom. He was bone tired, and he'd been up since dawn living through a day that had gone from bad to worse. How stupid could he be, bringing home a strange woman?

He'd just have to start over again tomorrow and hope it got better. First thing tomorrow morning he'd eliminate one of his problems. He'd have Madeleine Harmon's little behind on the seat of his truck right after breakfast.

If Jenna would let her go.

3

SOMEONE HAD SET the table for breakfast. He noticed three blue-checked place mats, paper napkins, silverware, and the brochure of the Ripple K propped up against the salt and pepper shakers. The cover caught his eye: "A Roundup of Vacation Pleasures." Stuart picked it up, opened the slick folder and saw, "A Western welcome awaits you." Maddy Harmon hadn't been given much of a "Western welcome" at the train station. He looked closer at the pictures of happy tourists riding horses around cactus and lounging near the pool, a foaming waterfall, and a photo of a bright dining room that served "hearty ranch-style meals."

He had to feel sorry for his houseguest. Frozen pizza wasn't exactly "hearty ranch-style" fare. Except on this ranch.

Stuart tossed the brochure back on the kitchen table and poured himself another cup of strong black coffee. He'd been up for three hours, since dawn, and now it was time for breakfast. Of course, he'd hoped to have a housekeeper who'd fix it for him. So much for planning.

"Good morning," Maddy said, stepping into the kitchen. She was dressed in jeans and a blue T-shirt and was almost pretty when she smiled, he decided. Her dark hair was tied back again, like last night. Stuart suppressed a sigh. She wasn't exactly housekeeper material.

"Morning," he managed. It had been two years since a woman had been in this house. Or had been in his bed. He frowned, uncomfortable with the thought. Usually hard work could make him too tired to care.

"I'm all packed."

He moved to the coffeepot. "Want some?"

"I can get it myself," she offered, her voice cheerful. "I'm not exactly a guest, am I?"

"No problem," he said, pouring her a cup. He handed it to her, trying not to touch her fingers as she took the mug. "Careful," he warned. "It's hot."

It was a good thing she wasn't his type, he realized. Yet, after two years, he'd practically forgotten what type he preferred.

"Thank you." She took a cautious sip and looked more cheerful. "I needed this."

"I was just about to make breakfast." He opened the refrigerator to prove that he had his mind on food. "Want some eggs?"

"Only if you let me make them."

He put the carton on the counter and looked down at her. "You won't get much of a fight from me."

"Really?"

That smile again. He backed up a step and put his hands up in a gesture of surrender. "Yep."

"Okay. How do you like your eggs?"

"Any way at all."

"I should have known that cowboys wouldn't be fussy." She opened the refrigerator and looked inside as if waiting for divine inspiration. Then she started removing vegetables and a couple of baked potatoes.

He sat down at the table and thought about removing his hat. "Guess this has been a strange start to your vacation."

"It sure has." She pulled a frying pan from the hanging rack above the stove and set it on the burner. Then she took a knife and started peeling a potato. "But a delay of one day isn't going to make any difference. I'll be horseback riding through the desert by this afternoon."

"At least you got to stay on a real ranch for one night."

"True, but the Ripple K is real, too."

"If you believe what you read." He tipped the hat back off his forehead. Guess there was no harm in asking. "I could get the pool filled."

She turned to him, but didn't stop slicing the potato pieces into the skillet. "What do you mean?"

"The only difference between their ranch and ours is whether you earn money or pay it out."

Maddy looked surprised, but she didn't say anything for a moment. Instead she picked up an onion and reached for the cutting board. The potatoes started to sizzle.

He tried again. "You could think about staying here, just for a week or two until I find a replacement. Or until Mrs. Abernathy can take the job after all."

"You don't even know me."

"I'm a pretty good judge of character." She looked doubtful, so he had to add, "You didn't throw a fit about landing in the wrong part of New Mexico, and you've had experience as a housekeeper. At least, that's what you said yesterday in the truck."

"I took care of my grandfather. Being a housekeeper wasn't exactly a profession."

"Well, I figure you're not a serial killer."

She smiled. "No."

"That's what I thought." He was pleased he'd made her smile. Now all he had to do was get her to agree to his plan. "I'll pay you what you were going to pay at the dude ranch. And refund whatever the deposit was."

"That's quite a bit of money."

He nodded. "It would be worth it. I have a ranch to run, and a daughter to raise. I need the help." Which was only half of it, but he didn't have to tell her his life story in order to have her work for him for a week or two.

"I know, but—"

"But you don't want a job."

"Nope." She opened cupboards until she found a bowl, then proceeded to crack eggs into it. She beat them with a fork, stirred the potatoes and onions in the frying pan, and then poured the eggs on top with a skilled motion. She rummaged through the lower cupboard, found a large lid, and plopped it on top of the pan. "There," she said, before turning back to Stuart. "I'm making us a farmhouse omelet."

"Never heard of it." Stuart knew he should be helping her but he was entranced by the capable way she took over his kitchen.

"Potatoes on the bottom, eggs in the middle, cheese on top." She picked up her coffee cup and joined Stuart at the table. "I appreciate the offer, really, but I was looking forward to all that 'riding the range' stuff."

"You can ride the range and wear your new hat here," he offered. "And get paid for it."

"Well, I have to say that's very tempting, but—"

"Here's the deal," he said, wishing he had an easy way with conversation. "You'd only have to cook two meals a day. We'll all make our own lunches. You'd have to do the grocery shopping, maybe help buy some new clothes for Jenna over in Deming. And I'll fill the pool. Can you swim?"

"Yes. I don't have my lifesaving certificate, but—"

"Good enough," he interjected. He didn't want to hear her objections. Not yet. "Jenna needs encouragement to read something other than horror novels. She's behind on book reports, but the school gave her the summer to catch up on her work. I already know you read."

"Mr. Anderson—"

"Stuart," he corrected.

"Stuart," she said, looking at him with a curious expression. "You keep interrupting me. I don't know anything about kids or their clothes. Or writing book reports. I really don't think I'm what you need."

He shrugged. "But you're all I've got."

She laughed, got up, and went to the stove. Before she picked up the pot holder, she turned back to him. "That's very true." She chuckled. "Hard to believe, though."

"Will you think about it?"

She seemed to hesitate, then said, "All right."

"For how long?" He couldn't hide his impatience as he watched her poke the omelet with a spatula. "I've got a ranch to run."

"Do you have any cheese?"

"In the refrigerator. There's a drawer." He started to get up to find it for her, but she found it before he could push back his chair. He sat down and watched her slice ribbons of Cheddar over the omelet, then cover the pan with the lid. "How long?" he asked again.

"Just a couple of minutes, until the cheese melts."

She put four slices of wheat bread in the toaster and pushed the lever down.

"I meant, how long until I know if you're going to stay."

"Oh. I can't think when I'm hungry. After breakfast," she answered. "I'd have to call the ranch and find out if I could get another reservation in two weeks. Is Jenna around?"

"She's outside. She usually fixes herself a bowl of cereal."

"The table is set for three people."

"Jenna must have done it."

"She has chores?"

"A few, outside. She'd be expected to help you with the kitchen chores."

"You're certainly trying to make this look easy."

"Nothing about Jenna is easy," he said. "I have to be honest about that."

Maddy simply smiled as the toast popped up. She brought the frying pan to the table and served him a hefty portion of the omelet, then put a slightly smaller one on her plate. "I appreciate that." She went back for the toast, put the slices on a plate and retrieved the butter dish before returning to the table.

Say no, the voice inside begged—the voice of a woman who wanted freedom and adventure. *Just say no. Get on with your exciting summer plans*. Maddy sat down, put her napkin in her lap and picked up her fork.

"Looks good," Stuart said, taking a bite.

She looked away. It was the oddest thing, sitting across the table from a handsome man. Especially a man in denim, wearing old boots and a faded button-down shirt with the sleeves rolled up. It was the fulfillment of every Western fantasy she'd ever dreamed of, and about as impossible to obtain.

"I hope you like it."

"I do," he said.

They ate in silence, with Stuart getting up once to refill their coffee cups. Imagine that—a man who poured coffee for her. She'd try not to let that affect her decision.

Financially speaking, Stuart's offer made sense and would give her an extra cushion in case of an emergency. On the other hand, this could be the only summer of her life when she didn't have to make a decision based on finances. She could do whatever she wished.

What she wanted to do was experience life on a ranch.

And the best-looking man she'd ever seen in her life was offering it to her. Was she crazy to leave or crazy to stay? Louis Grey's book had contained a grizzled old foreman and a handsome cowboy, but no children who were about to flunk out of elementary school. Maddy knew that she was no romantic, beautiful, impetuous heroine of Western novels, but surely she could pretend for two weeks. Fourteen little days. She could pretend this was her life, not some expensive stay on a guest ranch with fifty-nine other people who were pretending, too.

She fingered the brochure, and Stuart's lips thinned. She could pick an elaborately rustic dining room, with meals served to her. Or she could postpone all that and serve the "chow" in this overcrowded kitchen.

Maddy looked up at Stuart, forgetting the brochure she still held between her fingers.

"You'd have your own horse," he offered, his blue

eyes staring at her with a particularly intense expression.

She winced. "You're not making this easy."

"I don't intend to."

Maddy hesitated. "And a sunrise breakfast ride?"

He put down his coffee cup. "A *what?*"

"It's in the brochure." She read the words to him, "'A horseback ride before dawn, coffee at sunrise while watching a spectacular desert view.'"

"I'll find the view," he agreed, looking surprised that she would want to be up at dawn. "If you make the coffee. Is there anything else?"

"I'm not sure," she said, unfolding the brochure once again.

He leaned forward and took the folder out of her hand. "Lady, I may be desperate but I'm not crazy. Will you take this job or not?"

"I'll take it," she said, surprising herself with the words. Stuart Anderson might not be crazy, but Madeleine Harmon, 1990s spinster from Connecticut, might be. It would only take two weeks to find out.

"WHY DOES SHE HAVE a name like 'Snake'?" Maddy surveyed the chestnut mare tied to the corral railing and wished the horse was called "Lady" or "Majesty" or even "Desert Storm." "Snake" didn't quite fit the fantasy of what an adventurous woman should be riding the range on.

Jenna shrugged. "I don't know. She's always been called that."

"Oh." Maddy patted the mare's neck, and the horse turned to look at her with suspicious brown eyes. "She doesn't look too happy."

"Sure, she is. She likes a good ride. And she needs the exercise."

"Don't we all," Maddy muttered. The horse was saddled up and, according to Jenna, ready to go. Was New Mexico ready for this? She hadn't ridden a horse since she was twelve and spent two weeks at Girl Scout camp to earn her horse badge. She hoped it would all come back to her. Like riding a bike. Or playing bridge.

Jenna hopped on a sturdy black pony and waited for Maddy to climb on Snake, so Maddy untied the reins, stuck her foot in the stirrup, grabbed the saddle horn and swung herself onto the mare's back. Mission accomplished, she smiled at Jenna and adjusted her new hat. "What do I say now—yippee?"

Jenna giggled as Stuart leaned over the fence. "Not unless you're from Connecticut," he drawled. "Go ahead. *Yippee.*"

Maddy turned to see his long frame leaning against the fence, one booted foot hooked on the bottom rail. How long had he been there? "It was a joke."

He grinned, as if he didn't believe her. "Sure, it was." He stepped over the fence and stood next to Maddy. "Your stirrups okay?"

"Just right." She looked down as he ran his hand along the cinch, avoiding touching her leg. Then he gave the horse a satisfied pat and stepped away. "You ladies have a good ride. Just be back in time to go to town at two o'clock."

Jenna looked disgusted. "That only gives us three hours."

Stuart once again looked as if he was trying not to laugh. "Maddy needs to start out slow, don't you think?"

Maddy shot Jenna a look that said *Don't argue,* and

Jenna clucked to her horse. "We're wasting time," she muttered. "Follow me. We'll check on the cattle in the northeast section and see if anything's going on."

"Yippee," Maddy called, hoping to make the man smile again. His face was shaded by the hat, and she couldn't read his expression. Disappointed, she nudged Snake into following the black pony. The horse didn't need much urging, and her quick walk gave Maddy time to adjust the reins and accustom herself to the unfamiliar feel of a horse between her legs as they headed through the pasture and toward a rounded hill.

"Don't go too far, Jenna," Stuart shouted from behind them. "Take good care of Maddy. She's the only housekeeper we've got!"

Damn right, Maddy thought, turning her attention to the mountain scene in front of her. *At least for the next two weeks.*

"The Peloncillos," Jenna said, pointing.

But Maddy already knew that. After all, this particular mountain range had figured prominently in *The Lights of the Desert Stars*. She still couldn't believe she was seeing it in person, on the back of a horse named Snake. She drew her horse up beside Jenna. "This country is beautiful. Just like in the books I've read."

"Wow, no kidding? You think it's beautiful? I've never read a book about my own home before."

"You can borrow one of mine."

"Maybe."

"Just let me know whenever you want to read it." Maddy guessed that Jenna didn't like to commit herself to anything that could turn out to be something she wouldn't like to do. Lloyd Harmon, her grandfather, had been the same way so Maddy was used to it.

"Some of *Desert Stars* is pretty old-fashioned, but the part about the gold mine is really interesting."

"Gold mine?"

Gotcha, kid. "The Lost Mine of the Hermanas," Maddy said casually. "Have you ever heard of it?"

"Uh-uh." Jenna looked disappointed. "There are a few ghost towns near here. Maybe we could find out."

"Ghost towns?" Maddy was thrilled. She knew there were ghost towns but she didn't know they were close by. "Can we ride there?"

"No. Too far."

"Oh."

"You're doing great. Want to go faster?"

"How much faster?"

Jenna kicked her horse into a trot. "*This* fast," she said. "No big deal."

Snake trotted to catch up without Maddy giving her instructions, and within minutes she was able to adjust to the motion and feel fairly confident that she could stay in the saddle.

The scene at the top of the ridge took her breath away. There was something almost mystical about such a wide, empty expanse of space. Land stretched for miles, joined to a flat horizon and enormous sky. Maddy suddenly felt very, very small.

"Jenna! Wait up!" She reined in Snake and sat, trying to absorb the scene before her. To her right, the mountains rose up to the pale sky. Far to the north another mountain range was barely visible. The rest was just as she'd imagined, in golden colors of the high northern desert country she'd read so much about. She didn't want to rush through it. She wanted to savor every single minute, because this was as far away from Connecticut as Madeleine Harmon was ever going to get.

"What's the matter?" Jenna called, turning her horse so she faced Maddy.

"Nothing," Maddy said, kicking Snake to a trot. When she neared the child, she added, "I just wanted to look for a few minutes."

"There's nothing to see."

"Yes, there is. Especially if you're from Connecticut." Jenna didn't look convinced, but Maddy didn't care. She was suddenly filled with such an overwhelming feeling of happiness. If she didn't hang on to Snake's reins, she would float right off the horse.

"YOU HAVE A LIST?"

"Yes. A long one." Maddy moved very slowly toward the truck. After three hours on top of Snake, Maddy didn't know if she would ever be able to put her thighs together again. The hot water of the shower had only delayed the painful reaction. Now she just had to hope that her sundress hid the fact that her thighs were a foot apart. The blisters from her boots were covered with Band-Aids, making her grateful she'd brought along sandals.

"I brought the checkbook," he assured her. He frowned as he watched her waddle down the steps. "You okay?"

He'd noticed she could barely walk. Amazing. "Just fine," she said, trying to walk with her legs together.

"Guess two hours on a horse is too much."

"*Three* hours," she groaned.

"You don't believe in starting slow?"

"I don't have the rest of my life, you know. I'm on vacation." Then she realized what she'd said. "I'll be able to cook dinner tonight, if that's what you're worried about."

"What?"

She looked up at him as she caught up to him at the truck. "I'll be able to cook dinner," she repeated. "Don't worry."

"I meant," he said, with an irritating patience, "*what* are we having for dinner?"

"I took some steaks out of the freezer. I'll pick up other things at the store."

He nodded his approval. "Mac has an open invitation. Even if he doesn't come for supper, he'll probably show up later for dessert and coffee."

"No problem," she said, pleased to use his phrase. She climbed into the truck beside Jenna as every muscle protested.

"I don't feel good," Jenna said, clutching her stomach.

Her father started the engine. "We haven't even left the ranch yet."

"It's just a feeling," she explained. "I always get it. All I have to do is *think* about riding in the truck."

"You need sunglasses," Maddy said, pulling a pen out of her purse. "I'll add that to the list."

Stuart turned the truck around and started down the road. "Think you can drive this?"

"Sure, as long as I don't have to throw a saddle on it." *Or spread my legs in front of the steering wheel.*

"Good. It's not hard to get to Lordsburg, then after that Deming." He turned onto a wider road. "Take this road to 9, then a left on 338 to 10. East on 10 to Deming. You'll find everything you need there."

She'd have to take his word for it. "You'll draw me a map for next time? I can get lost anywhere."

"Sure."

The three of them were quiet all the way to town.

Jenna clutched her stomach, Stuart drove, and Maddy looked out the window and wished she'd brought her camera. She'd never seen so many miles of flat land. This was the "real West," all right.

Stuart parked the truck in the middle of town and looked around at the array of stores. "New clothes for Jenna first," he said, climbing out of the truck. He was tired of those ripped jeans she liked to wear, and if he never saw that faded green T-shirt again, that would be just fine with him. He didn't know why his daughter dressed like a three-hundred-pound bag lady, but he was paying Maddy to fix that situation, at least.

The three of them went into the first clothing store they came upon, and Stuart stood awkwardly near the door as Maddy and Jenna started looking through the racks of clothes.

"What about something like this?" Maddy held up a pink jumpsuit.

"That's fine," Stuart replied. "I have an account here. They know Jenna."

"No way," Jenna said. "I hate pink."

"With your coloring..." Maddy saw a stubborn expression cross Jenna's face and put the jumpsuit back on the rack. "You're right," she said. "It's not very practical."

"I like jeans."

Stuart came closer, his hat in his hand. "That's all you wear," he growled. "Makes you look like I don't bother to buy you anything."

"I *like* jeans," Jenna argued. "All the kids wear jeans."

Maddy held up a pair of colored denim shorts. "How about jean shorts? Cute, huh?" The girl looked dubious, but Maddy didn't give her a chance to protest. "And these V-necked T-shirts in pretty colors. *Not* pink, but light blue?" She held up one. "And yellow?"

"Maybe."

Maybe was quite a concession. Maddy looked at the saleswoman, who gave her a sympathetic look. "The girls are all wearing these cotton shorts," the woman said, stepping closer. "With matching shirts, of course. These striped ones are very popular."

Maddy didn't give Jenna a chance to say something negative. She directed her to a dressing room, tossed an assortment of summer clothes inside and shut the door. "Come out when you have an outfit on so I can see how it fits and what size you are."

Silence. Finally the child said, "These shorts are too big. No way am I coming out."

"I have to see how big, so I can get another size."

"I'm not coming out."

"Okay. Are they a lot big or a little big?"

"I don't know."

"Oh, hell," Stuart muttered. "This kid is crazy."

"Shh." Maddy pulled him away from the dressing area, behind a sock display. He wasn't easy to budge, she realized, feeling the iron muscles beneath her hand. Not an unpleasant feeling. She tried to keep her mind on shopping and off cowboy muscles. "She's not crazy," she explained. "She's just growing up. Isn't there something you have to do in town? Besides stand around here, I mean?"

He looked down at her. She thought she saw those light eyes twinkle, but she wasn't sure. "You trying to get rid of me?"

"Yes. For a while."

He put his hat back on his head. "An hour?"

"Make it an hour and a half. This could take longer than I thought."

"Meet you back at the truck." He looked at the dressing-room door. "Good luck."

She waved him away. "Don't worry. I shop better than I ride."

"Thank God."

She laughed, leaving him standing beside the bright rows of pastel socks. He turned and headed out the door. He felt like he'd been rescued. Maybe he hadn't done too badly, after all. He didn't get the housekeeper he expected, but Jenna seemed content. Maddy appeared to be competent in that area, anyway. He smiled as he thought of the way she'd tried to hide the fact that she'd spent too much time in the saddle. Tourists! Too many people had seen the movie *City Slickers*. He'd had a few laughs at that one himself, but it sure showed how many people in the world still wanted to live the cowboy fantasy and ride off into the sunset.

Stuart looked at his watch. He had time to buy a newspaper and a cold beer. That beat shopping, any day.

MADDY WAS READY TO DROP dead after shopping with the stubborn eleven-year-old for two hours. She wondered why she had ever agreed to taking the job. Someone should have warned her that shopping with a girl was *hard*. Actually, Stuart had tried to warn her.

At least he'd been honest. She'd have to give him credit for that, anyway.

She was tired, sore, hungry, thirsty and still had the grocery shopping left to do. And they were running thirty minutes late, but there'd been no way she could outfit a picky preadolescent in ninety minutes. Especially one who didn't want new clothes in the first place.

She'd assumed girls liked shopping. She'd never met one who didn't, but then again, she hadn't known too many. The little girl next door had always seemed pretty happy.

Stuart had charge accounts in every store in town, or at least Miss New Mexico had. The late Mrs. Anderson must have been quite the shopper. Maddy hoped she would see a picture of her sometime, although one look at Jenna was most likely all she'd needed to see the girl's mother.

"We're done, right?"

"Yes," Maddy answered, sounding just as relieved as her little companion. "You're all set with clothes for the rest of the summer."

"Think Dad will like them?"

So the child wasn't as tough as she pretended to be. "I'm sure he will."

"Good," Jenna said. "Then he'll get off my case about *that*, anyway."

Maddy crossed the busy street beside Jenna and headed toward the truck. She could see Stuart's tall frame leaning against the door. "That's one way to look at it."

"I'd rather buy food," the child said. "Wouldn't you?"

"Since I started working for you and your father, I don't have much of a choice." Maddy chuckled. "I have a feeling you two are going to keep me very busy."

"Is that good or bad?"

Stuart walked around to the passenger side of the truck and opened the door. "Well, Jenna," Maddy said slowly, admiring the tall rancher's impressive shoulders, "I think it's probably pretty good. What about you?"

Jenna rolled her eyes. "I think you have a lot to learn."

"And you're going to teach me?"

"Yep. Me and Dad."

4

FIVE STEAKS AND BAKED potatoes should have been easy to fix. Trouble was, Maddy decided, no one left her alone and everyone had a better idea on how the food should be prepared. Jenna declared she didn't know why they had to bother with a salad, especially since she was the person assigned to shred the lettuce. Mac told her five times that he liked his steak fried, not broiled. And Stuart stayed out of the way, except to suggest no one *really* needed vegetables, at least not tonight.

And no one was on time except Mac. After her salad chore, Jenna disappeared and had to be called for dinner three times, and finally Stuart hauled her out of her bedroom. Then he got a phone call and went into the dining room and talked for fifteen minutes while she tried to keep the steaks at medium-rare and not well-done.

It wasn't easy, but no one had told her it would be.

"What'd y'all do in town?" Mac drawled, watching Maddy cover the steaks with aluminum foil. "What are you doing that fer? Some fancy Eastern way to cook meat?"

"No," Maddy answered, glancing toward the kitchen entry as if she hoped Stuart would be standing there. "I'm just trying to keep these steaks warm until Stuart is through with his phone call."

"We bought clothes," Jenna told him. "Not too dorky. They're okay."

"Shoot," the man said to Maddy. "He won't be off any time soon. That boy has bulls to sell."

Was that an expression that meant her boss talked a lot? She must have looked confused, because Mac explained, "It's his business. He sells cattle. Buys cattle. Raises cattle. You get too many bulls and you've got to sell some. And people like Triple J bulls."

"Yep," Jenna agreed. "They sure do. Where are the chips? Didn't we buy some?"

"We did, but we're not eating them now," Maddy said. "We're having dinner. As soon as your father sells a bull, that is."

"Dad always lets me have chips and salsa before dinner."

"Well, I'm the housekeeper and in charge now. No chips. No salsa. At least, not tonight." That was another strange thing. They wanted to pour salsa on everything. Hot salsa, the kind that should be labeled, "Eat this and you run the risk of bursting into flames."

Jenna frowned. "What are we having?"

"Steak, potatoes, French bread and salad."

Mac's face fell. "No dessert?"

"I picked up a peach pie and vanilla ice cream. How does that sound?"

"Like heaven, Miss Maddy." The old cowboy smacked his lips. "Like heaven."

Miss Maddy? Madeleine had never been called that before, but it had a Southern flavor she decided she liked. If Mac wanted to call her Miss Maddy, it was all right with her.

"What's heaven?" Stuart drawled, stepping into the kitchen. "Did I miss something?"

"Yes," Maddy said, pointing to the table. "You've almost missed dinner. Have a seat."

"We're waitin' supper on you, son," Mac complained. "Those steaks are gettin' cold."

"Sorry." Stuart sat down at the table and scooted his chair forward.

Maddy quickly put the food on the table and then sat down beside Jenna, which put her directly across from Stuart. Every muscle in her body ached as she moved, and sitting on the hard wooden chair didn't help, either.

"Need a cushion?" Stuart asked.

Maddy shook her head, shifting gingerly on the seat. "No, I'm fine."

Stuart turned to his daughter. "Get Maddy a pillow. Her, uh, bottom is a little tender."

Maddy flushed. She wasn't used to anyone, especially a handsome man, referring to her rear end—another strange thing about New Mexico. Jenna returned with a dark red pillow, and Maddy had no choice but to lift up and tuck it under her.

"Better?" Stuart's eyes twinkled, as if he sensed her embarrassment.

"Yes, thank you. Now, I think we should eat before everything gets cold. You can pass the steak platter, and I'll serve the salad."

Jenna speared a baked potato. "What are we going to do tomorrow, Maddy?"

"I'm not sure." She looked at Stuart. "Is tomorrow a good time for the sunrise breakfast ride?"

Mac frowned at Stuart as he took the platter of meat from his hand. "What the hell is a sunrise breakfast ride? Some dude-ranch thing?"

Stuart ignored the man next to him and attacked his

steak. "You sure you're going to feel up to that tomorrow? Don't you want to give, uh, yourself time to heal?"

Maddy sliced open her baked potato. "Maybe you're right."

"Take a short ride tomorrow, break in easy. You probably are sore in places you didn't know you had."

Actually, she was sore in places she knew she had, but had never used, but she would swallow salsa before she'd admit it to the sexy cowboy across from her. She turned to Jenna. "Any other ideas?"

"We could ride out to see Tom and Cindy."

"Too far," her father said. "You don't want to cripple the housekeeper, remember."

Jenna turned to Maddy. "How long is it going to take you to get into shape?"

"I hope not very long. I only have two weeks."

The child looked slightly appeased. "Okay. We're gonna hafta work on it."

"You have other things to do than ride all over New Mexico," Stuart warned his daughter.

"Like what?"

"Your reading list."

"That dumb thing?"

Stuart looked at Maddy as if to say, *See what I'm dealing with?* "It's only dumb if you have to repeat fifth grade."

"I won't go back to school," Jenna cried. "And you can't make me!"

"Don't threaten me, young lady. I—"

"My grandmother had a helpful rule," Maddy interrupted. "Anyone want to hear it?" She looked at the others, who didn't say anything, so she took that as a sign that they were interested. "She wouldn't allow arguments at the dinner table. She said it interfered with the digestion."

"So when did you fight?" Jenna asked.

"After dinner, or during dessert. We had some lively discussions, but while we were eating we tried to avoid subjects that would start arguments."

Stuart looked aggravated. "Is that a hint?"

"Just a suggestion."

"Meaning," he said, leaning forward, "that Jenna's lack of reading skills should be discussed at another time."

"Yep." Very Western, saying "yep" like that. Maddy vowed to use it more often.

"And what would you like to talk about during dinner?"

"How about a history lesson? I'd like to know more about this area. There were Indians, right? And wars with Mexico?"

"And gold mines," Jenna added. "Don't forget about that."

"Gold," Mac muttered. "There's a lot of stories about New Mexico gold."

"I have time," Maddy urged.

Stuart shook his head. "Watch out, Mac. The Easterner here will be getting gold fever. She'll wander off into the mountains with a donkey and a pick and never be seen again."

"Tell us a story," Jenna urged. "Was gold found in the Peloncillos? Maddy has a book about it."

"Fiction, Jenna. It made for a good book, but that doesn't mean it's true."

"The Lost Mine of the Hermanas," Mac muttered.

Jenna's gaze flew to Maddy. "That's it! That's the one, isn't it?"

"Yes." She looked at Mac. "That mine really existed?"

Stuart put down his fork. "Would someone pass me the bread?" He took the basket from Mac. "See, I told you not to start this. I don't want to lose a valuable housekeeper to gold fever."

"I'm only temporary," Maddy reminded him. "After this, I could become a treasure hunter."

Jenna grinned. "Can I do it with you?"

"We'll see," Maddy said. "If you have time for gold hunting, you have time to read."

"Come to think of it, there might be some old books in the bunkhouse," Mac drawled. "I'll have a look around."

"Ridiculous," Stuart said. "You want gold, go to the jeweler's in Deming. That's about all the gold you'll find in this area."

"If it makes the women happy," Mac insisted, "then they should search for whatever they want."

"I'd also like to learn how to fish."

"Women don't fish," the old cowboy sputtered.

"Why not?"

Stuart leaned back in his chair. He grinned at the old man. "Now it's your turn to try and talk her out of something."

"Well, if that don't beat it all! Women fishing!"

"What's wrong with that? I bought waders from the Cabela's catalog."

"Waders! Damn!"

"I don't know what's wrong with women fishing," Maddy said, unperturbed. She finished the last bit of her dinner. It had been pretty good, if she did say so herself. She had grown used to going without meat.

Having a freezer full of the homegrown variety was quite a luxury.

"Ain't natural, that's all."

Maddy ignored him. She didn't mind his bluster. In fact, he reminded her of her grandfather, which was the nicest surprise of the summer so far. She got up and started clearing the empty plates from the table. "You can have dessert right now, or wait until later. Give me time to make a fresh pot of coffee and a pitcher of iced tea to go with the peach pie and ice cream. Seven-thirty okay?"

Stuart almost smiled, which for him meant he was thrilled. He glanced at his watch and stood. "Seven-thirty is fine. I have to meet with the boys and find out if they got that fence fixed."

"Those college kids? They couldn't fix their—"

"Mac," Stuart warned.

The old man rose, too. "I'll just go with you, then." He turned to Maddy. "Thanks for dinner, ma'am."

"You're welcome." She looked at Jenna. "You're excused, too."

The girl's expression brightened. "I don't have to help with the dishes?"

"Not tonight. You helped with the grocery shopping, so go on out and play until I call you."

"Thanks, Maddy!"

Maddy was left in the room all by herself, which was a form of heaven, she decided. She sat back down at the table, gingerly replacing the cushion under her bottom. If anyone had told her that she would be happily washing dishes on a New Mexico cattle ranch this summer, she would have laughed them right out of her grandfather's little bungalow and into the Atlantic Ocean.

MADDY ROSE AT SIX the following morning, unwilling to waste her vacation hours sleeping. Someone—Stuart, she supposed—had already made the coffee and drunk half a pot. The house was quiet, so Maddy poured herself a cup of coffee and strolled through the house. She didn't quite know where to start.

If she was going to get paid for being a housekeeper, then she'd better start acting like a housekeeper. First of all, she'd ask Stuart if she could move his papers into another space. Breakfast and lunch were fine for the kitchen, but she'd like to use the dining-room table for supper. She'd eaten in the kitchen all her life, and now here she was in a hacienda with a dining room large enough for twenty people. Something so grand should be used. She bet Mrs. Abernathy would have had the furniture polish out within minutes of moving in.

The problem was knowing what the housekeeper could do and what she couldn't do. She took her coffee and went to the front door to find her boss. Stuart was leaning against a fence, deep in conversation with a younger man. A green pickup truck sat near the larger barn, and two young men hung around it, as if waiting for someone to tell them what to do. She sipped the strong coffee and watched Stuart and the young man shake hands before he drove off. The two younger men stood listening to Stuart, then went into the barn. Stuart headed toward the house, looking preoccupied.

He stepped inside and stopped, as if surprised to see a woman in his house.

"Good morning," she said.

"Morning." He tipped his hat back. "You're up early."

"I'm supposed to be working, right?" She smiled.

Again, he looked surprised. "No hurry. You can make your own hours."

"I'm making breakfast," she said. "Just give me a few minutes."

"No hurry," he repeated, as if awkward with the new relationship.

As they approached the dining area, Maddy asked, "I'd like to serve dinner in the dining room from now on, if you don't mind."

He didn't seem to be paying attention. "Do whatever you want."

"But what about—"

"Look," he said, stopping to look down at her. "You're the housekeeper. You run the house. You make the rules. If I don't like them, I'll tell you, but until then, run things your own way. Just see that we all get fed and that Jenna reads every day, writes her book reports and stays out of trouble."

That was a long speech for the rancher. "Fine," Maddy said. "What do you want for breakfast?"

He sighed. "You make it, I'll eat it. Fair enough?"

"Fair enough." Maddy shot one longing look at the table piled high with papers. She knew what she would do after breakfast.

It didn't take long to fry a couple of eggs and six sausages. Of course, he put salsa on everything on the plate except the four pieces of whole-wheat toast. She'd never seen anyone eat so much. But she'd been feeding a sick old man for the past few years, so what did she know?

He looked up from the destruction of his breakfast. "Aren't you eating anything?"

Maddy filled up one of the sinks with soapy water. The counters were going to get a good scrubbing before she tackled the dining room. "I'll have something later."

"If you're going to ride, you should ride in the morning. Try to avoid the afternoon heat."

She squeezed the excess water from the sponge and attacked the countertop. "All right. I'll find Jenna and see where she wants to go today."

"I called someone about the pool. You should be able to swim this afternoon."

"I'm sure Jenna will be happy."

"Yep. She has certainly taken a shine to you."

"I don't know why—I don't know much about kids," Maddy admitted.

He drained the rest of his coffee. "Maybe that's the reason. You don't treat her like a little kid, and yet you don't expect her to act like an adult."

"She must miss her mother very much."

Stuart stood and put his hat on his head. "Thanks for breakfast," he said, leaving the kitchen in two long strides.

Maddy turned back to her counters. Obviously it was not a good idea to mention Jenna's mother. Was Stuart Anderson so filled with grief that he couldn't talk about his wife even two years after her death?

Jenna ran into the kitchen and opened the refrigerator. "I don't eat eggs," she informed Maddy. "Just cereal. I'll fix it myself."

"Fine."

"What are you doing?"

"Cleaning."

"This place isn't dirty."

"It isn't clean, either," Maddy said. "I need to start earning my money around here." She tossed the sponge in the sink and watched Jenna fix herself a bowl of cereal. "Here's the deal," Maddy told the child. "We ride in the morning. Or something else very Western and adventurous. Afternoons we read, write, and all that. Swimming before and after the reading. Then you're free until dinner, at six."

Jenna didn't look thrilled, but she didn't argue. "Okay, I guess."

"Good. We'll start today." Maddy had it all figured out. Early mornings she would clean, fix breakfast, and plan the evening meal. By ten she'd be free for some of that Western atmosphere she longed for, and at the same time keep Jenna occupied. "You can show me your book list."

Jenna made a face. "You'd think I was gonna *die* or something if I don't read those books."

"Wouldn't you hate to have to go back to school and not be in the same grade as all of your friends?"

"I don't have any friends."

"Why not?"

Jenna shrugged. "Dad doesn't let me invite anyone over."

"You've never had a girlfriend over here?"

"No."

Maddy's eyebrows rose. Maybe Jenna just needed to reach out to the other girls. And maybe her father needed to learn about raising a daughter.

STUART EYED THE THICK envelope with his attorney's name imprinted on the upper left-hand corner. His in-laws weren't going to stop, that much he was sure of. He stuck his thumb inside the flap and ripped it open, then pulled out the sheaf of papers. It didn't take long to put the pieces together: the Newmans didn't think he was a fit parent and were suing for custody of their granddaughter. They wanted Jenna, and considering the way they'd raised her mother, Stuart would fight them every inch of the way. Now, they were getting serious. There would be a hearing, his lawyer informed him. A hearing to decide whether Jenna would live with her grandparents in Los Angeles permanently.

"Over my dead body," Stuart muttered. "That's the only way they'll get that child."

He'd loved Jenna since he'd first seen her—a chubby two-year-old with blond ringlets and big blue eyes. She'd looked just like her mother, only Jenna's angelic expression was real. He hadn't known Connie long, but he'd felt sorry for her, trying to raise a child by herself. He wanted to be a father, wanted children to pass the ranch to someday, like his father and grandfather and great-grandfather had. Certain he'd finally found the woman of his dreams, he'd been putty in Connie's conniving hands.

He'd been in for one hell of a shock. Connie had delayed getting pregnant for over a year, and then informed her husband she had no intention of ruining her figure again. She liked to spend money, liked to drive fast and especially loved to flirt with other men when she thought her husband was too busy to notice. He'd put his foot down more than once, but it hadn't done much good.

He'd finally given up.

So, here he was, fighting the Newmans. It wasn't enough he'd spent seven years fighting with Connie. Now he had to fight for Jenna.

Well, he thought, stuffing the papers back into the envelope. He'd fight, all right. There was no way in hell he was going to give up his daughter.

"YOU'VE GOT A LOT TO learn around here," Stuart warned Maddy. He saddled Snake and checked the cinch. "So take it easy. Don't get overanxious."

"But—"

"But nothing," he said, stepping back to let Maddy mount. "Don't let Jenna talk you into any more three-hour rides."

"I'm not so sore today," she fibbed. Her blisters wore triple Band-Aids and still stung.

He looked as if he didn't believe her, but he couldn't argue. "You've been here less than forty-eight hours. You have another—"

"Twelve days," she supplied.

"Twelve days," he continued, "to live out your Annie Oakley fantasies. I'm just telling you I don't want you to get hurt while you're doing it."

"Annie Oakley?" Maddy started to laugh. "No one would ever mistake me for her."

"No kidding," Jenna said, a grin on her face.

"Jenna," he warned.

"That's okay." Maddy chuckled. "I can take the teasing. I'm just going to turn into such a great rider that you're not going to believe I wasn't born in New Mexico."

Father and daughter didn't look convinced, so Maddy added, "I could be entering rodeos by September, maybe win one of those big silver belt buckles. Garth Brooks will present it to me, in person."

"Well," Stuart drawled, "you can shoot the bull like a cowboy—I'll give you that much."

"Thank you, Mr. Anderson." Maddy tipped her hat to him. "That's a start."

"From 'yippee' yesterday to silver belt buckles," he said. "Are all Easterners like you?"

Maddy shook her head. "If they were all like me, they'd be out here."

"Which is why there are so many guest ranches."

"True." She picked up the reins. "Have any more advice for us?"

"Head south," he said. "Get a glimpse of the Coronado in the distance."

"Isn't that a state forest?"

"I'll drive you up there one of these days," he offered. "For today head south and take a look around." He turned to Jenna. "You have the compass?"

She patted her saddlebags. "And water and sunscreen, too."

Jenna nudged her horse into a trot, and Maddy followed her lead. This time she felt more accustomed to Snake's gait as they rode behind the corrals and up a gentle rise. Maddy didn't even care what particular scenery she saw; just being in New Mexico and on the back of a horse was nothing less than a miracle. Her camera was on a strap looped around her neck so she was ready to take pictures. She surveyed the expanse of land that lay before her. There was certainly nothing disappointing about New Mexico scenery.

When they returned to the ranch hours later, the increase in temperature was noticeable. Yesterday Maddy had been too excited to care, but now she could see why people were careful in the afternoons. Jenna showed her how to care for Snake, and once the horses were rubbed down, Maddy and Jenna headed for the house.

Stuart stood on the wide front porch talking to two young men. Both of them tipped their hats when Maddy walked up the steps.

"Bill and Joel, meet Miss Maddy Harmon, from Connecticut. She's the housekeeper here."

"Ma'am," they said in unison. Their gaze slid back to Stuart, obviously curious as to what the relationship was.

Stuart seemed totally oblivious, and continued discussing the northwest range as Maddy murmured, "Nice to meet you," and went into the house.

"Well, do we eat lunch or shower first?" Maddy asked.

"Eat," Jenna replied with no hesitation.

"Fine with me." They went into the kitchen and made thick ham sandwiches from the ham Maddy had bought at the store. "I'll meet you at the pool in half an hour. Bring the list of books."

Jenna rolled her eyes but didn't argue. Maddy decided that had to be an improvement.

"WHAT THE HELL—" Stuart stopped and stared. The dining-room table was totally devoid of anything remotely resembling paperwork, except for the napkins that were placed to the left of each plate. "Maddy!"

"What?" She popped out of the kitchen. Her cheeks were flushed, and her hair was on top of her head in a ponytail. Somehow she didn't look like a housekeeper at all, but more like a woman. Stuart took a step backward.

"Where's my office?"

"I moved it." She looked terribly pleased with herself.

"You moved it," he repeated slowly. "Why and where to?"

"I explained to you this morning. You told me that I was the housekeeper and to do my job." She tossed the dish towel over her shoulder and walked down the hall to face him. "So, I'm doing my job and serving dinner in the dining room."

"This hasn't been a dining room in..." He hesitated. He couldn't remember when they'd last used it. Connie had given a few parties, but how long ago was that? "In years," he stated emphatically. "*Years*."

Maddy didn't look at all surprised. "I asked myself, 'What would Mrs. Abernathy do?'"

"What in hell does Mrs. Abernathy have to do with this?"

"She'd be the real housekeeper."

"If she ever gets here," he muttered.

"Well, I don't know about that, but since I have the job, I thought I'd do it right."

"Where are my papers?" He didn't want them lying around where Jenna could find them. He hadn't told her about the custody battle and didn't intend to. The kid had had enough upsets without worrying over where she was going to live.

"I moved them to the spare room next to mine," she said. "It was empty and even had a desk and a phone jack."

Stuart frowned. He'd grown used to having his papers spread out near the door. He looked at Maddy and wondered what he'd gotten himself into, after all.

"Go back and look," she said. "You might like it." She turned and went back toward the kitchen, as if expecting him to follow. Stuart frowned. She was wearing that pink dress again and looked too feminine for a ranch hand. Damn, it made him uncomfortable.

Maddy returned to cutting up vegetables while Stuart went through the kitchen and into the other wing, past Maddy's room and into the spare bedroom. He looked in to see his papers stacked neatly on the desk and the bed. The room looked as if it had just been vac-uumed. Through the long windows the pool sparkled and beyond, another miracle. Jenna lay curled up un-der the porch eaves, reading a book. A hardcover book.

Stuart turned back to the doorway of the room. Well, it might not be so bad using this for a while. Just for a while. He didn't know why it was so important to eat in the dining room, but if that's what Maddy wanted, that's what he'd do.

It was a small price to pay for a happy daughter and a home-cooked meal.

5

"THIS IS *SO* WEIRD." Jenna stood near the table, Mac and Stuart next to her. Maddy peered through the pass-through, delighted to see that the sliding panel worked so well.

The three residents of the Triple J stood in the dining room as if they didn't know what to do next. "What's the matter?" she called. "Don't you want to sit down?"

Stuart looked around for her voice. "I see you found the old serving panel."

"It's great. I figured it would be easier than carrying everything around the corner."

"Where do you want us to sit?"

"Anyplace you want," she sputtered. "It's your table. Take the head."

Stuart sighed, and pulled out his chair. He didn't look as if he enjoyed the "lord of the manor" role. Maddy turned back to her dinner. Pot roast, cooked this morning and chilled, arranged in slices on a heavy clay platter. A huge bowl of pasta salad, and thick slices of whole-wheat bread, compliments of the freezer section of the supermarket. Wide wedges of cantaloupe completed the meal.

Jenna peeked through the opening. "Can I help?"

"Absolutely," Maddy told her. "You can take this platter and put it on the table."

Little hands grasped the platter and disappeared.

Maddy took the pitcher of iced tea and put it through the opening in the wall, then she went around the corner to the dining area.

She eyed the lace-covered table with satisfaction. "I found the table linens. What do you think?"

Stuart didn't smile. "I feel like Ben Cartwright on 'Bonanza.'"

Maddy went over to the serving counter and started retrieving the rest of the meal. "Is that good or bad?"

"Good," Mac answered.

"Bad," was Stuart's reply.

"You two better make up your minds." She took the seat beside Jenna, across the table from Mac. There were enough chairs for five more people.

"Hell," Stuart said. He stood and picked up his glass, then moved to the seat beside Mac so the four of them faced each other.

"Thought you was going back in the kitchen to eat your dinner," Mac said, not trying to hide his chuckle.

"I didn't want to be left out of the conversation," he said.

Maddy moved the bowl in front of her. "I'll serve the pasta salad. Mr. Cartwright?"

Stuart half smiled, and he lifted his plate to be served. "Thank you, ma'am."

"You're welcome." She put several scoops on his plate, then looked at Mac. The old man didn't look very excited. "Mac? What's the matter?"

"What's that, some fancy Easterner food?"

She looked at the bowl filled with cooked macaroni, olives, chopped vegetables and Italian dressing. "I guess you could call it that." He lifted his plate, and Maddy gave him a sample. "Try it. You might like it."

"I don't like olives," Jenna said.

"Pick them out," Stuart told her. He turned to Maddy, who passed him the platter of meat. "Dinner looks real good."

"Thank you." Maddy put her napkin in her lap and handed Jenna the basket of bread.

Stuart's eyebrows rose. "You baked bread?"

"Sort of. I bought frozen loaves, thawed them and put them in the oven." She fixed herself a helping of salad, then passed the other dishes to Jenna. She glanced across the table at Mac and Stuart. They looked pleased with the food. At least they weren't complaining, unless you counted Jenna's aversion to olives. "Have you thought any more about when we could do the sunrise ride?"

Stuart looked up from his plate. "Well, no, I—"

"What about tomorrow?" Jenna suggested.

"Well, I don't—" Stuart looked at both of them, then shrugged. "I don't see why not."

Mac chuckled. "Got you cornered, son. Nowhere to run."

"No, I promised." He looked at Maddy and nodded. "That was part of the deal. Besides, any woman who can make a meal like this deserves to have her promises kept."

Maddy smiled back at him, ridiculously pleased by the warmth she saw in those blue eyes. This housekeeper business might just be easier than she thought. It was going to be hard to remember that this wasn't a vacation, after all.

THE STARS WERE everything Louis Grey had described. Alluring and mystical, they called to her, much as they had called to the heroine in the book. Their light reflected off the water in the pool, sending their magic sparkling between the two wings of the hacienda. Maddy, in shorts and a baggy T-shirt, stepped onto the veranda and slid open one of the doors to the quiet courtyard.

She should be in bed; after all, it was close to midnight and she'd been up since six. But she couldn't afford to waste a minute, and here were the stars calling to her to admire them.

She went closer to the pool and sat at its edge, dipping her feet into the tepid water. It was about twenty degrees warmer than the Atlantic Ocean, a fact that she had appreciated when she and Jenna had gone swimming this afternoon. The heat was different here, dry and windy. No moist, humid air to contend with, but no cooling breeze from the ocean at night, either.

She liked it, though. She sat for long minutes and realized she wasn't the least bit homesick. She would need to buy postcards to send to a couple of the neighbors. And souvenirs for herself, to remember the desert. She would fib and write, "Wish you were here. Miss you."

A shadow fell near her, and she turned to see Stuart approaching. He held two thick glasses.

"Can't sleep?"

"Didn't want to," she replied, telling herself that she shouldn't feel as if she was trespassing.

"Here." He handed her one of the glasses. "I made a couple of margaritas. Figured you should have something authentic to drink."

"Thanks," she said, surprised that he'd thought of her. "I didn't hear you in the kitchen."

"I wasn't. There's a bar in the living room," he said. "Behind the panels east of the fireplace."

"Oh. Guess I'll have to clean it one of these days."

She sipped at the drink. It was tart, salty, and very cold. "What's in this?"

"Tequila."

She took another swallow. "It's good."

"It'll help you sleep." She saw his smile. "Why did you really come out here, Maddy?"

She thought about his question for a long moment. "I came out here for a vacation," she answered. "To see the West."

"How old are you?"

"Twenty-eight."

"Never married?"

"No. Engaged once." She didn't know why she told him that, except for her pride. She didn't want him to think she'd never had a date. Or never been in love. Just because she'd never tasted a margarita didn't mean she hadn't lived.

"Recently?"

"No." She smiled, feeling the pleasant numbness as the alcohol started to take effect. "I'm not out here recovering from a broken heart, if that's what you're wondering."

"Tourists go to Tucson or Phoenix or Santa Fe, instead of here, in the middle of nowhere."

"Tourists go on sunrise rides, too."

"We're leaving at five," he said.

"I know. I have the alarm set for four o'clock."

"You sure you want to do this? We're talking about a couple of hours, at least, one way."

"I can't think of anything I'd enjoy more."

He didn't look convinced, but he didn't argue. "Put the food in a couple of sacks in the morning and I'll pack it up."

"Coffee and sandwiches okay?"

"Fine."

"I'm not really very sore anymore, either." She smiled again. "I thought I'd never be able to sit down again."

"At this rate you'll be working the rodeos before you're thirty."

"The oldest living cowgirl?"

He nodded. "Yep."

"Maybe I will. I'd like to do it all."

"You sound like someone who's been set free," he said, studying her over the rim of his glass.

"Well, maybe you're right, cowboy," she drawled, feeling the effect of stars and tequila. "And I don't think I'll ever go back to the way things were before."

He gave her a strange look, and drained his glass. Then he backed away, as if uncertain how to reply to her openness. "You can have a job here as long as you want."

She shook her head. "Thanks, but two weeks is all I can spare."

"You've been a big help already."

"Thanks." She finished her drink and climbed to her feet. "I'm glad I could help."

"See you in a few hours." He reached out and took her glass.

"Thanks for the drink."

"Have to treat the help right."

"You have." He went into the house through the living-room doors, and Maddy turned in another direction, toward her room. Stuart Anderson was an interesting man, to say the least. She hadn't expected to meet a man like him.

Stop fantasizing, Harmon. A man like that has other things on his mind. The only thing he needs is a housekeeper.

Somehow that thought was disappointing.

"MORNING." Stuart appeared out of the darkness. Leading two horses, he looked very much the Western rancher, with his denim shirt sleeves rolled up to reveal brown forearms. He wore old jeans, dusty boots, and the ever-present cowboy hat. It wasn't that clean country-and-western singer look. He looked as if he was ready to do a hard day's work.

Which, Maddy was certain, didn't include taking a tourist from Connecticut up to the mesa for a cup of coffee.

"You ready?" he asked, glancing at her zipped jacket and jeans.

"Good morning," she answered. She'd just finished saddling up Snake the way Jenna had taught her yesterday. "I *think* we're ready."

He turned to the horse. "You saddled her yourself?"

"Yes. She was very patient."

"Snake's a good horse. Been around here a long time." Stuart checked the saddle, gave the horse a pat and then swung the leather bags over Snake's rump. "I think you brought enough food," he said.

"I hope so. I really wasn't sure—"

"I'm teasing," he said, turning to her. "From the weight of it, I'm sure there's plenty. You can mount up. Jenna will be along in a minute."

"What about Mac?"

"I told Mac where we were going, and he said he'd think about joining us, but not to wait for him."

"I guess he decided to sleep in."

"Yeah. He's doing a lot of that these days."

She swung herself into the saddle. "I didn't see Jenna this morning."

"She was pretty sleepy, but once she remembered where we were going she woke up fast."

"You don't do this often?"

"No. This is a special occasion." He shot her a reassuring smile. A smile that disappeared as fast as it came.

Jenna came running across the yard. "Wait up!"

"We're not leaving without you," Stuart said. "But we'd better get a move on if we're going to be on the mesa before dawn breaks."

On the mesa before dawn breaks. Maddy sighed with happiness. That sounded so Western. She wanted to memorize it, so one day when she an old woman she could say she had been up to the mesa before dawn. For coffee. With one of those strong, silent-type cowboys.

And if there was one thing to say about Stuart Anderson, it was that he was silent. They mounted their horses and, with Maddy in the middle and Stuart leading, they wound their way around the ranch and up into the low foothills beyond. There wasn't much to see, although the sky was growing almost imperceptibly lighter.

They climbed, up through the brushy foothills and higher to where the air was cool and dry, and the breeze blew the scent of pine around them.

Maddy's stomach growled. She'd eaten a piece of toast before she'd gone out to the barn, but nothing else. Now she wished she'd eaten something more. She watched Stuart guide his horse around the brush and copied every move he made. She didn't want to mess up her first horseback ride with him. Maybe Connecticut greenhorns didn't get second chances.

She glanced at her watch. They'd been riding for almost forty-five minutes, and the sky was still dark.

"How are you doing?" Jenna called.

"Great."

"Sore?"

"No." Maddy shook her head. "I'm over that now," she fibbed. Actually, her thigh muscles were starting to feel the strain already.

She kept telling herself it would be worth it. And she'd be in great shape for all of the activities on the Ripple K. Why, she'd put the rest of the guests to shame. After all, she could saddle her own horse now, she already owned a hat, and her new jeans smelled like leather and horse sweat instead of a department store.

Not a bad start.

It was still too dark to take pictures, but not dark enough that she felt as if she was riding at midnight. The time went by fast. When Maddy next looked at her watch, almost an hour had gone by. They rounded another ridge, and Stuart turned to look at her.

"There's your desert," he called, pointing to his left.

Maddy urged Snake forward, and when she drew up next to Stuart she looked across a wide expanse of flatland that threatened to take her breath away. Dim gray light rose from the eastern horizon, warning of the approaching sun.

"We just made it," Stuart said, swinging off his saddle.

"My goodness," Maddy breathed. "This is going to be incredible."

Jenna frowned. "It doesn't look like much to me."

"It will," her father promised. "Give it a few

minutes." He turned to Maddy and put his hand on Snake's bridle. "You getting down?"

"Sure." She dismounted slowly, pleased that her legs cooperated by supporting her. It was always better not to fall flat on your face in front of your boss.

"I don't know about you ladies," he drawled, "but I'm ready for coffee and breakfast."

Maddy turned back to the horizon as the yellow glow lit the sky. She looked in the opposite direction, which was still dark.

"It's even better at sunset," Stuart said. "The western sky has more colors."

"Can we come back some night?" Jenna asked.

"Not by yourselves," he told her.

"You'll take us again?"

"We'll see. How about that coffee?" he asked, lifting the saddlebags from Snake's back. "Is anyone hungry?"

"I am," Maddy answered, trying to ignore the easy way Stuart lifted the heavy bags, and the way he took that strength for granted.

"Me, too," said Jenna. "I could eat a bear."

Maddy reluctantly turned away from the tall rancher. "How about a ham-and-cheese sandwich instead?"

"Okay."

Maddy helped Stuart unpack the saddlebags, finding the banged-up thermos and plastic cups. They took everything out and Stuart pointed to a large rock. "Watch out for rattlers," he warned.

"In the rocks?" Maddy took a step backward.

"Especially the rocks," he said, taking a blanket and spreading it on the ground. "This works fine. Sit."

"You sure? This isn't a joke?"

"As sure as it gets," he replied, unscrewing the lid of the thermos. So Maddy sat, looking around the area for coiled snakes. Rattlesnakes hadn't fit into her Western fantasy at all. She took the cup he handed her and set it on the blanket while she found the sandwiches and passed them out. She also set out apples, the leftover melon wedges from dinner and a foil-wrapped container of brownies.

The three of them faced east, watching silently as the yellow streaks mixed with peach and the blazing yellow sun lightened the wide sky.

She didn't mind Stuart's silence or Jenna's noisy appreciation of the breakfast picnic. Once the sun hit the sky, it rose rapidly, showering the desert with its bright, searing light. It was everything she had read about, and Maddy felt her grandfather's approving presence. He would have been happy to know she'd followed his instructions and headed west.

"This is totally awesome," Jenna said with a sigh.

"Yes," Maddy agreed. "I can't believe I'm sitting here on top of the world."

Stuart's lips lifted into a smile. "I guess that's a good way to describe the Continental Divide."

Jenna sidled closer to him. "Have you been up here before?"

"Yes."

"How many times?"

He dug the heel of his boot into the dirt. "I wouldn't know."

"Well," she persisted, "when was the last time?"

There was a long silence, then he replied, "After my father died. I came up here to think."

Jenna sighed. "I wish I could have come here after Mom's accident."

Maddy held her breath, wondering what the man would reply. The child obviously wanted to talk about her mother. Couldn't Stuart see that? But, to Maddy's frustration, Stuart didn't say anything, and neither did Jenna. The sun blazed upon them, and Maddy leaned back and snapped a picture of the man and the girl facing the sun.

"WELL, DID YOU AND the women get the sun up?" Mac grinned as he walked into the barn.

"Yep, sure did." Stuart slipped the saddle off his horse. "Didn't you notice?"

"And you had your little picnic?"

"Yeah. What's so funny?"

"You are, Anderson." He came closer and took the bridle off the horse. "You're just about the funniest thing I've seen all mornin'."

"Yeah?" Stuart tried not to encourage him. Mac was the biggest tease on the ranch, and Stuart had spent much of his childhood ducking the old man's jokes. Between his father and Mac, Stuart had learned that the less said, the better, because the two men could make a joke out of the most innocent remark and torture him with it.

"She's not a bad-looking little gal." Stuart ignored the old man, so Mac continued, stepping closer. "And a good cook, too. Even if she expects us to eat in that dining room like some damned cattle barons."

"She's the housekeeper," Stuart reminded him. "I told her to do what she wanted, and if I didn't like it I'd tell her."

"And you didn't tell her." Mac chuckled.

"No reason to. A little polish won't hurt Jenna. That's what I want for the girl."

"A woman's influence."

"Yeah."

"The Newmans still trying to take her away?"

Stuart ignored the tightening in his gut. "Harder than ever."

Mac shook his head. "A woman's touch wouldn't do *you* any harm, either, son."

"I don't—"

"Don't try to tell me no different," he ordered. "I know what I'm talking about, and even though Connie put you through—"

"I don't want to talk about her."

"All right." The old man nodded. "Well, you went and got yourself quite a housekeeper, all right."

"She'll do. For now." Stuart almost smiled. He hadn't expected to admire the way Maddy's little bottom bounced on the saddle, or to want to touch the curling hair that dropped down from beneath that oversize cowboy hat. She had no idea how ridiculous she looked in that hat, or how appealing.

He didn't want her to look appealing. He wanted her to look like someone who was good at vacuuming. However *that* looked. He wanted her to be over seventy years old. And maternal. Very maternal. Grandmotherly, even.

"For now, huh?" Mac grinned and shook his head. "I forgot, she's only stayin' a couple of weeks. Well. Not enough time for a slow mover like you."

"I'm not making any moves."

"A woman's touch, son. Have you forgotten what that's like?"

"No," Stuart muttered. "I haven't forgotten a whole lot of things."

"Not all women are like the one you married. I could have warned you, but you wouldn't listen."

"My mistake."

"At least there's Jenna. She's a good girl, just a little high-strung right now. Them hor-mones, you know."

"Yeah," Stuart agreed, hiding his smile. "I know."

"Madeleine will settle her down. After all, a girl who reads Louis Grey has to be something special."

"She's going to help Jenna with her reading."

"That's good. Long as they don't start trying to hunt up a gold mine."

"You never know."

Mac spat in the straw. "That's right. With women, you just never know."

SHE DIDN'T KNOW WHAT was the matter with her. Maddy stirred the cooking ground beef, chopping it with the edge of the metal spatula and mixing in the diced onions.

Of course, she winced; she had a few sore muscles. That had been quite a ride this morning. It had been after ten when they'd arrived back at the ranch, and she'd taken a shower and then vacuumed the house, including the bedrooms.

Stuart's had been disappointingly stark. Oh, a few framed photographs of people she assumed were his parents, and Jenna's school picture, but none of Connie Anderson, Miss New Mexico. Ivory carpet, ivory walls, a huge dark wooden bed and bright Navajo blankets on the walls, but nothing more personal. She'd told herself she wasn't interested as she'd pushed the vacuum cleaner around the room. She'd peeked through an adjoining door to see an enormous bathroom and closet area. She'd debated whether or not to clean it, but it had looked fine. She would ask Stuart first. Something told her he'd consider it an invasion of privacy.

Jenna's room was different: identical carpet and wall colors, but her bed was a white iron twin topped with a blue-checked bedspread and a mountain of pillows. Maddy had made the bed, arranged the pillows carefully against the headboard, and picked up a mound of dirty clothes from the floor.

She'd fulfilled her other duties, too. She'd met Jenna at the pool for their swim and book-report discussion. Jenna had decided to read one of Maddy's Western novels, but since the author's name was not on the list of approved reading material, they'd had to compromise. Jenna would have to begin reading a book for school. As soon as she finished that, she could read a Western in her "spare" time.

Tonight Maddy would have to ask Stuart what else he expected of the "housekeeper" for the next eight or nine days—unless Mrs. Abernathy showed up. Maddy frowned at the browning beef. Somehow the thought of Mrs. Abernathy didn't make her feel any better.

Maddy poked at the beef. She wondered if they'd like her version of shepherd's pie for their dinner. Melons were in season, as well as berries, so she'd fixed a large bowl of fruit salad and stored it in the refrigerator. Biscuits from a can, and instant mashed potatoes on top of the layer of chili-flavored meat would complete the meal. They'd eat it; of that she was sure.

Later she'd go over Jenna's book report on the mystery novel and see if it was acceptable—as if she'd know. She wanted to talk to the sixth-grade teacher to find out if the girl was on the right track.

But there was more to Jenna's problem than just entering the sixth grade. There was something between her and her father. Stepfather, that is. Stuart was the only father Jenna had ever known, but a death stood between them. Jenna needed something her father wasn't giving her, and tonight Maddy resolved to talk to her new boss. It was time to start asking a few questions. For instance, what had she gotten herself into?

Just then, the man with the answers walked into the kitchen.

"Smells good," he offered, stepping toward the refrigerator. He opened it and pulled out a cold beer. "Want one?"

"Sure. Your chips and salsa are on the table over there." Maddy watched him twist the tops off the bottles, then he stepped closer to hand one to her.

"Thanks." She took the skillet off the burner and started spooning the grease into a bowl while Stuart sat down at the kitchen table. She looked over at him and wondered how he could put in such long days and still look so good. He tilted his hat back off his forehead, and reached for a chip.

"You joining me?"

She brought her beer over to the table and sat down. "I need to talk to you about a few things," she said. "I vacuumed the bedrooms today. I'm assuming you want me to clean the bathrooms and do the laundry, too, right?"

He frowned. "When I hired you I guess I was thinking more about the cooking and taking care of Jenna."

"A housekeeper would have to make sure the house was clean," Maddy suggested. "At least, that's what I'd think, if I hired a housekeeper."

He didn't look convinced. "You're not here to clean bathrooms."

"What about the laundry? I don't know where the washer and dryer are."

"There's a stacked unit behind folding doors in the hallway near my room."

"I thought that was the linen closet." Maddy took a swallow of the beer. She was starting to develop a taste for the stuff. No more tasteful glasses of white wine for Maddy the Mesa-Roving Cowgirl.

"No. That's in your wing." He helped himself to a generous amount of salsa on the tortilla chip. "Where's Jenna?"

"Reading, I hope. This is her time for independent study."

"And she's doing it?"

"Yes, so far. That's something else I wanted to talk to you about. Is there someone I can call, someone at the school, to find out if I'm doing the right thing with Jenna's reading?"

"It's summer vacation."

"Surely there must be someone I can talk to. Who is her sixth-grade teacher going to be?"

"I'm not sure. Jack Patterson, maybe. I'll give you the phone number for the school."

"Great." Maddy went over to the counter and wrote the names down on a piece of paper. She'd call first thing in the morning, and if that didn't provide the information she wanted, she'd call the teachers at home. Surely they wouldn't mind answering a couple of questions. "I know I'm only going to be here for nine or ten days longer, but if Jenna can get on the right track, maybe she can stay on it."

"You don't have to leave," he said, his expression serious.

Oh, yes, I do. Maddy shook her head. "You should

give Mrs. Abernathy a call. Maybe she's all set to come now."

"I could tell her I already hired someone."

Maddy returned to the chair and faced those gorgeous blue eyes above suntanned cheekbones. His eyebrows were dusty, and she had the strangest urge to run her fingertip across them and smooth the frown lines. "I can't stay," she murmured.

"Of course you can."

"No."

"For the summer," he insisted. "I know you don't want to be a housekeeper for the rest of your life, but another eight weeks can't matter."

Maddy looked at him and wondered if he had any idea what he was asking. Not matter? She was such a gullible, squishy-hearted person that she would end up browning hamburger and slicing fruit on this ranch for the next fifteen years. She had to be careful. She had to stay strong.

Maddy sat up straight, took another swallow of beer, and looked Stuart right in the eye. "It matters," she declared. "I've been taking care of people all my life, and it's time for a change."

"You sure?"

She nodded. "Absolutely," she declared, wondering why leaving didn't sound like any fun at all.

6

STUART ANDERSON DIDN'T give up easily. Ask anyone. He'd never quite given up on his marriage, even though he should have. He wouldn't give up his daughter, and Jenna was *his* daughter. He was the only father Jenna had ever known, and that counted for something. Damn right, it did.

And he wanted Madeleine Harmon, would-be cowgirl from Connecticut, to stay on the Triple J as housekeeper.

Hell, he didn't mind eating in the dining room. And he didn't miss the layer of dust all over the furniture, or the microwaved burritos for supper or Jenna's sullen silences. He wasn't sure what kind of magic Maddy used to make the house run so well, but he wasn't going to complain.

She liked the pool; he'd have one of the boys clean it every morning. He remembered what it had been like last night, sitting near her by the side of the pool, the stars reflected in the clear water. The surprise in her eyes when he'd handed her the margarita had pleased him. She wasn't used to men waiting on her, that was for sure. She was no beauty, but she had a certain soft appeal. He couldn't put it into words, and he wasn't about to try.

So now Stuart Anderson, man of the West, was going to try to convince Maddy Harmon to stay on his ranch. In other words, abandon her vacation plans, save her tourist dollars, and roll up her sleeves.

He would use the Western stars and the desert sky and the mountain view—in other words, he was going to pull out all the stops to keep her on the Triple J.

He mixed a pitcher of margaritas, glancing around the corner to make certain Maddy still sat by the pool. He'd sneaked a nap in the bunkhouse this afternoon—twenty minutes, with his hat over his face so no one dared ask him any questions. But Maddy had been going strong since before dawn, so he'd better get out there now while she was still awake.

The night air was warm as he pushed the door open with a booted foot.

"Aren't you tired?" he asked as he approached her, then wished he'd started off with something more welcoming.

She turned around. He saw she wore a bathing-suit top and light-colored shorts. Her curling hair was loose, falling to her bare shoulders. Her breasts swelled above the swimsuit fabric, surprising him with their tempting roundness. He tried to keep his mind on his mission.

"Yes," she replied, a slight smile on her face. "But it was such a special day that I guess I'm not ready to have it end."

He handed her the drink. "Thought you might like this. It can kill the pain if you're sore from the ride."

She took it. "Thanks, but I think I'm starting to get in shape."

She was in shape, all right. He tried not to look at her chest. Why had he thought she was plain?

"The morning was wonderful," she continued. "I

don't know if I thanked you enough, but that sunrise is something I'll always remember."

"There are sunsets, too," he said, sitting next to her by the edge of the pool. Her feet were in the water, but he wasn't the least bit interested in copying her. He wasn't much of a swimmer, or even a toe dipper.

"Yes, from the front porch. Mac told me, but I haven't had a chance to watch the whole thing."

"Tomorrow," Stuart ordered. "You'll have to watch one from start to finish."

She sipped her drink. "Sounds good to me."

It was time to try again. "This is a good place to live," he said, hoping he sounded casual.

"Jenna is very lucky to be able to grow up in a place like this. Most kids just dream of living on a ranch."

"I don't think Jenna thinks it's so great."

"Sure, she does."

"It doesn't show."

"She's at an awkward age," Maddy explained. "Give her some time."

"What about you? Did you dream of ranches and mountains and deserts when you were a kid?"

"Oh, I sure did. I read Westerns, tons of them, and dreamed of riding the range on a splendid black horse." She shook her head and took another sip of the drink. "It took me enough years to get to this part of the country."

"What happened along the way?"

She shrugged, the expression in her eyes mysterious and sad. He had the sudden urge to put his arm around her and hold her to him, but he resisted. She'd probably go screaming off into the Peloncillos, which was not part of his plan.

"College," Maddy answered after a long moment.

"A sick grandfather and a broken engagement." She looked at him and smiled. "In other words, reality."

His voice was dry. "I've heard of that."

"I think it happens when you least expect it."

"Did the sick grandfather have anything to do with breaking the engagement?"

"Just about everything. I gave up a good job in an accounting firm to go home and take care of him. He'd suffered a stroke, and there was no way of knowing how long he'd live."

"No one else in your family helped you out?"

"No. It had been just the two of us for a long time. I knew he needed me, though, and that was really all that mattered."

"And your fiancé didn't agree."

"No. He'd counted on my salary to finance some business deals, and when that wasn't going to happen, he found someone else."

"That kind usually does," Stuart commented. *The son of a bitch.*

"That was three years ago," she said. "Now I can look back and be glad I didn't marry him. He'd just been using me. It had nothing to do with love."

"Most things don't," he stated.

"I don't think that's true. No matter what, I don't think I can be that cynical."

Stuart didn't look convinced. "Not cynical. Realistic, remember?"

"If that's true, I don't want to be realistic, either." She drained the rest of her drink. "I should be careful with tequila," she said. "It makes me talk even more than usual."

He chuckled. "I came out here to talk to you."

"Uh-oh."

Stuart rattled the ice cubes in his empty glass. "This might be a two-margarita conversation." He stood and plucked the glass from her hand. "Don't move. I'll be right back."

Don't move? She didn't know where else she'd rather be. Under the stars with the handsome rancher, her feet in the tepid water and the warm glow of tequila drumming under her skin. Hey, this was the stuff dreams were made of. Maddy tipped her head back to look at the stars. Acres of them, miles of them, a universe full of them. All shining down on New Mexico and the Triple J and Madeleine Harmon.

Stuart returned in a few short minutes, and once again the thrill of being waited on almost made her speechless. Of course, the key word was *almost*.

"You're going to ask me about staying on as housekeeper again?" she asked, taking the drink. "Thanks," she said, appreciating the way the cold glass felt against her hand. "I guess I won't have any trouble sleeping tonight after I drink this. Although I might have a little trouble getting up in the morning."

He sat down near her. "I didn't make yours strong."

She licked some of the salt from the rim of the glass. "I could get used to this."

"That's what I'm hoping, of course."

She told herself to be strong. To stand firm. "It won't work, Stuart." She liked using his first name.

"Look, what happened at the train station was an accident."

She smiled. "You're telling me?"

His mouth relaxed slightly. "Jenna likes you."

"Liking me doesn't have anything to do with it. That child needs a father, not a housekeeper," Maddy said. "She thinks you don't want her around, you know."

He set his glass down, and his mouth tightened into a thin line before he spoke. "What in hell would make you say a damn fool thing like that?"

"She told me," Maddy replied, pleased that he would be so angry. He must care. She knew he had to, no matter how he kept his feelings hidden. Or why.

"She can't believe that."

"I don't know, but I think she does." Maddy leaned forward. "That sunrise ride meant more to her than to me, you know, because she was with you. She needs to talk about her mother, and how much she misses her. She needs friends her own age." Maddy wished the stupid rancher would stop staring at her as if she'd stung him with a branding iron. "She needs a *haircut*, for heaven's sake."

"What does this have to do with her *hair?*"

Maddy shrugged. "I'm just trying to tell you that your daughter needs more than just a housekeeper."

"A woman's touch," Stuart said, echoing Mac's words of the morning.

"That helps, but besides the new clothes and getting her hair trimmed, she needs to know she's loved. She needs to know somebody, *you*—cares."

He drained his drink in three long swallows, and then got up. "Who says I don't care?"

Maddy took a deep breath and stood, too, so she wouldn't have to look up too far. Little beads of water ran down her legs and pooled on the cement. "No one is saying you don't care," she muttered. "Just that it doesn't show."

He stared down at her, his silver-blue gaze dark and unreadable. Maddy stared back up at him, wondering what on earth he was thinking. Whatever it was, it didn't look as if it pleased him.

When he bent his head she stopped breathing. She knew she was holding her breath and wondered if she'd ever breathe again as his cool lips touched hers. His fingers touched her chin, holding her mouth in position as his mouth moved against hers. It was an exploration, a question that Maddy didn't have the answer to; gentle in its approach, shocking that it happened at all.

When he finally released her, he lifted his head but still kept one rough finger under her chin. "I'm not good with words," he said.

She released her breath. What did words have to do with anything?

"I apologize," he continued, his voice low. "That shouldn't have happened."

"It shouldn't?"

"No," he said firmly. "I promise that if you stay here on the ranch, that kind of thing will never happen again. You're perfectly safe here."

He dropped his hand, as if suddenly remembering he still touched her. He picked up both glasses and started to walk away, but then stopped and turned. "I came out here tonight to convince you to stay on here. Think about it."

She nodded, and watched him walk across the courtyard, open the door to the living room and disappear inside the dark house. How could such a large man move so quietly?

It had been such a long time since she'd felt a man's touch, a man's exploring lips on hers. She didn't know if it was Stuart's effect on her, or if any man would be able to make her insides quiver when he kissed her under the light of the desert stars.

That kind of thing will never happen again, he'd said.

Well, that was a disappointment. She would give up her genuine snakeskin cowboy boots just to have it happen one more time.

HE DIDN'T KNOW WHAT had gotten into him. Or worse, he did know. Damn. He could blame it on the stars, he supposed. Except he'd never thought of himself as a romantic kind of man.

Not even close.

But there was something about her that really got to him. Maybe it was the open expression in her brown eyes, or the way her hair curled against the nape of her neck. She had a dimple in her right cheek that peeked at him when she smiled. And she smiled a lot.

He'd never met anyone so happy. Not that he minded, but all that cheerfulness coming from one person was pretty unusual. And disconcerting until you had time to get used to it.

He had to figure out some way to compete with a dude ranch. Hell, what could be better than living on a ranch and getting paid for it? Money was one hell of a factor, but it didn't convince Maddy to stay past the two weeks she'd promised. There were only a few days left in which to talk her into it. Stuart shut his bedroom door and frowned at the silent room. Money wasn't the answer, so what was?

"WHO'S YOUR BEST FRIEND?"

Jenna looked up from her bowl of frosted corn flakes and shrugged. "Why?"

Maddy poured herself a cup of coffee and sat at the table opposite the child. She'd need to make a fresh pot; she was having trouble waking up today. Maybe it was the sunrise, maybe the margaritas, maybe it was lying awake wondering why Stuart had kissed her. "I thought you might want to invite a friend over. Especially now that the pool is filled." She watched the girl's expression change to surprise, then disappointment.

"I don't think anyone could come."

"Why not?"

"I like Melissa Allen a lot, but she told me her mother won't let her come over here because there's no supervision."

Maddy considered that for a moment. Melissa Allen's mother might have had a point, considering Jenna's independent life-style. "Well, there is *now*."

Jenna stared at her, a hopeful expression lighting her blue eyes. "You think?"

"I'll call Melissa's mother myself. Today."

"I have her phone number."

"Great." Maddy sipped her coffee and decided she might as well go all the way. "Is there anybody else? We could even have a pool party."

"We could?"

"I'll check with your dad, but I can't see why he'd mind."

"He's awful busy."

"I know, but your pool party isn't going to affect him one little bit. Because *we're* going to do all the work."

"I don't think it's gonna be work. I think it's gonna be fun."

Maddy smiled. "Me, too. You give me a list and I'll take care of the rest. We'll try for Saturday afternoon."

Jenna jumped up. "Okay!"

"Finish your breakfast first." Maddy laughed. "I'm not doing anything else until I've finished my, uh, fifth cup of coffee."

"*Fifth?*" Mac entered the kitchen. "It's eight-thirty. How long you gals been up?"

"Too long," Maddy answered. "If you have a few minutes, I'll make a fresh pot."

"Sounds good," he said. "You seen Stuart around this mawnin'?"

Maddy shook her head and went over to the coffee-pot. "He hasn't been in for breakfast yet." It didn't take long to assemble the ingredients for another pot of coffee. "I'm making pancakes and bacon, Mac. Would you like me to fix you a plate?"

"Well," the old man drawled, leaning back in his chair and crossing his booted feet at the ankles. "That sounds tempting, Maddy. I'd like that." He looked over at Jenna, busy spooning cereal into her mouth. "How come you're eatin' frosty flakes when you could be eatin' hotcakes?"

"I like this better." She quickly finished her cereal and took the empty bowl and spoon to the sink. "I'll make the list," she said, and hurried out of the kitchen.

"What's with her? She's in a bigger hurry than a jackrabbit."

Maddy opened the refrigerator and took out the bowl of pancake batter. "She's going to have some friends over for a pool party. I think it will be good for her."

"Well, well," the old man drawled.

She turned on the heat under the cast-iron skillet. She didn't stop to wonder why she felt so at ease with the man. He reminded her of Lloyd Harmon, but even more, he was the foreman character in *The Lights of the Desert Stars*, almost as if he'd come to life just for the two weeks Maddy was in New Mexico. "What does 'Well, well' mean?"

"Means nothing," he replied. But he grinned. "Only a woman would think of havin' a party, with all them little gals runnin' around."

"It'll be fun." She heard the front door open, and her heart beat a tiny bit faster. Must be all that caffeine, she reminded herself as Stuart's footsteps clicked against the tile. He hesitated in the wide kitchen doorway. "Mornin'," he said, first to Maddy and then to Mac.

"Good morning. You're running late today?" Maddy asked, taking two mugs from the cupboard and filling them for the men. Stuart sat in his usual place, hooked his hat behind the chair and leaned back as Maddy put the mug in front of him. "Thanks, but I could have gotten it myself."

"That's okay," she managed, wishing she didn't feel so pleased to be within a foot of him. She quickly took a step backward as Mac muttered his appreciation. "Breakfast will be ready in a minute."

"Hotcakes," Mac informed him. "And bacon."

Stuart took a cautious sip of the coffee and frowned at the old man. "You shouldn't be eating bacon."

"He shouldn't?"

"Doctor said he had to watch his cholesterol."

Mac looked so stricken that Maddy hurried to reassure him. "I broiled it, Mac, so that the fat drained out. And I've drained it on a paper towel. But I guess bacon really isn't something you should have every day."

"I don't have it at all," he grumbled. "Along with a lot of other things."

Stuart and Maddy exchanged an amused expression. Maddy found it hard to look away, but the brief smile he shot her relaxed her stomach muscles. It was okay about last night; it hadn't changed anything, thank goodness. Maddy reluctantly turned away and began pouring circles of batter into the skillet.

Stuart cleared his throat. "Would you like to see a ghost town?"

She turned around in surprise. "What? Are you talking to me?"

"Yes. A ghost town. Called Shakespeare. It's been restored, and as far as I know it's open for tours."

"It sounds wonderful." More than wonderful, actually. More like fantastic.

"We can go on Saturday. I think they're open on weekends."

"I don't think we can go this Saturday. Jenna's going to have some friends over for a pool party. That is, if you don't mind."

"I don't mind, if Jenna doesn't. She never seemed real excited about having anybody over before."

Maddy debated whether or not to tell him the truth about that, then decided it was best to level with him. "I don't think the other mothers were comfortable with their daughters being here without, uh, someone to supervise."

He shot her a sharp look. "I see."

"Can we go Sunday instead?"

"We'll drive up there today," he stated. "After breakfast. I've given the boys their instructions for the day." Maddy saw the pancakes bubble. She quickly flipped them over and turned back to Stuart. "I'd like that."

"Did the Ripple K offer a tour of Shakespeare?"

"No. At least, not that I know of."

"Good."

She opened the oven and, using tongs, grabbed

pieces of bacon and put them on the two waiting plates. "What are you doing, collecting points?"

"In a way. It's part of my plan."

Mac hooted his astonishment. "You? Planning on being a tourist?"

"I want a housekeeper," he growled. *I want Maddy.* Even voiced silently, the thought startled him and made him turn away from her so she wouldn't see the words somehow imprinted on his forehead. He glared at Mac, who grinned back at him. "And my house-keeper wants to see New Mexico."

"How many points do you think a ghost town will give you?" Mac asked.

Maddy arranged the food on the plates and brought them over to the men.

"Aren't you eating?"

"Next batch."

"Fifty?"

"Pancakes?"

"Points."

She couldn't keep from laughing. "I don't need a job."

"What are you going to do after your vacation?"

She sighed. "Look for a job."

"That's my point."

"I'm a bookkeeper. Or at least, I was."

Mac swallowed a mouthful of pancakes. "Good pancakes," he said. He shook his fork at the younger man. "You need more than a new foreman. You could use a bookkeeper, from the mess your accounts are in."

"What would you know about my accounts?"

"I tried to do them, remember?" He turned to Maddy. "Gave up."

"Maddy moved my office."

"Where'd all that sh—uh—stuff go?"

Maddy finished pouring another round of pancakes into the skillet. "In the room beside mine. You need a foreman, too, Stuart?"

"Yeah. Tom and Cindy have been handling that part of the ranch now. But I'm going to have to hire someone for around here."

Mac pushed his plate away. "Tom's doin' a good job, too. You been out there to see?"

"Not this week."

"You should. His wife is one hell of a rider. Fries a mean steak, too."

"For an old retired man, you sure cover a lot of ground. And you shouldn't be eating too much fried steak."

Maddy laughed. "Here," she said, setting another platter of pancakes on the table between them. "Finish your breakfast so I can see a ghost town."

Mac speared three pancakes and released them on his plate. "Anything for you, Miss Maddy." He shot Stuart a mischievous look. "Right, Stuart?"

Unfortunately Stuart didn't even flinch. He turned to Maddy, an intense expression in his light eyes. "That's right," he agreed. "Whatever Maddy wants is fine with me."

Hoping he wouldn't be able to read her mind, Maddy turned back to the stove. What *did* she want? She wanted to see the West, and she was living on a ranch. She wanted a vacation, and instead she'd found herself working for the handsomest cowboy she'd ever seen. Not that she'd seen any, actually. But even if she'd met five hundred cowboys, Stuart would still be the best looking.

She didn't know what she wanted, she realized, as

she poured the last of the batter into the skillet, but she wouldn't complain if Stuart Anderson took her in his arms again.

"WE'LL GO SOMEWHERE else," Stuart declared.

"Is there more than one?"

"There has to be," he growled. They sat in the front seat of the battered truck and stared at the Closed sign. The town of Shakespeare, said the sign, was open on the second and fourth weekends of each month.

This wasn't even the right day of the week.

"Wait a minute," Maddy said, rummaging through her tote bag. "I have some brochures in here somewhere."

He eyed the lumpy flowered bag that took up a large amount of the front seat. "Yeah, I'm sure you do."

She ignored his sarcasm, instead pulled open her New Mexico guidebook. "I should have looked at this earlier." But she'd been too anxious to head to Shakespeare before Stuart changed his mind and decided to rope cattle or clean up his office or something. As it was, there had been seven phone calls for him before they could leave the hacienda and climb into the truck.

"Well?"

"Wait a minute," she said. "I'm looking up ghost towns in the index."

He reached across her and opened the glove compartment. He pulled out a much-folded map. "Here. This should tell us something."

"Here's one. Steins," Maddy said. "It's labeled as a ghost town on this little map." She leaned across the seat to show it to him, but at the same time he leaned toward her to point to something on his map.

It seemed inevitable that their shoulders touched and their maps bumped.

"Oops," Maddy said, dropping her guidebook. "I've lost my place," she stammered, as the book slid to the vinyl seat. She bent down to pick it up, then turned back to him. "What were you saying?"

"I don't remember." He tipped his hat back from his forehead and released his grip on the map.

Maddy cleared her throat. "I found another ghost town."

He reached over and plucked the sunglasses from her face, placing them carefully on the dashboard. "I said I wouldn't do this again," he muttered.

"Do what?" She knew what.

"Kiss you," he replied, hooking his index finger under her chin to lift it. "I'm breaking my promise."

"That's okay," she managed, before his lips claimed hers. Her hands found their way around the warm skin of his neck and clung there.

Stuart wanted to be gentle, he really did. But the touch of her fingers on his skin sent sensations that were anything but gentle coursing through his body. His extremely starved body.

Heaven, he decided, tasting her lips, urging her to part them so he could delve deeper. He wanted more than a sweet kiss in the starlight, but kissing her in the parking lot of a ghost town was less than romantic.

His body didn't care where he was. And romance didn't enter into it. He dropped her chin and gripped her shoulders, holding her against him so she wouldn't pull away. Not that she would, with her arms wrapped around his neck and his tongue exploring the sweet recesses of her mouth. She seemed surprised, he thought for one fleeting second, and not at all afraid of him.

And she kissed him back. Her tongue teased and danced with his, and he grew achingly hard in reaction.

It was an endless, drugging kiss; one that Stuart had no intention of ending anytime in the near future. Until a car horn blasted through the silence. He lifted his mouth from hers, smiled down into her dazed expression.

"Is someone honking at us?"

"Yeah."

She looked past him to see a yellow-haired woman in a dusty black pickup truck. "She's coming this way."

"She?" He turned to look.

"Stuart? Stuart Anderson?" the woman called, slamming her truck door behind her as she crossed the dusty parking lot. "Is that really you?"

He groaned, and turned away to roll down his window. "Margaret?"

She grinned, her short tousled hair tangling around her face as the wind lifted it. "It's been ages. I'm not even going to ask what you're doing here," she said. "Whatever it was looked pretty interesting." She shot Maddy a curious glance.

"I'd like you to meet a...guest of mine, Madeleine Harmon."

"Hi," the woman said. "I'm Margaret Jackson. I went all through school with Stuart, here, so I guess I have the right to tease him. Nice to meet you." She looked at Stuart. "What are you doing here? The place is closed today. In fact, it's only open two weekends a month."

"I know that now," he replied. "I wanted to show Maddy a real ghost town."

"Come back," she said. "Not this weekend, but the one after that. I'd see if they'd let you in anyway, but I don't know if anyone's home. I stopped by to pick up some info for the Chamber of Commerce."

"That's okay. We'll find someplace else to see."

"What about the Lunas Mimbres museum in Deming? Or the Blue Teal vineyards. If you like wine, it's supposed to be excellent. Where's Jenna? Peggy wants to have her over. Maybe they could go to the movies or something."

"She's fine," Stuart said, turning the key in the ignition. "Don't let us keep you, Meg."

Maddy leaned past Stuart toward the open window. "Jenna's having a pool party on Saturday afternoon. Would your daughter like to come?"

Margaret hesitated. "Just girls?"

"Yes."

"Okay." She shrugged. "Some of the kids have been having boy-girl parties, and I guess I just can't deal with that."

Stuart nodded. "Neither can I."

"I'll have Jenna call your daughter," Maddy promised.

"Great. Nice meeting you."

"You, too."

Stuart rolled up the window and backed the car around, then headed down the road.

"Nice woman," Maddy said.

"One of the best." He glanced over toward her. "She's been married to the same man, an old friend of mine, for twenty years."

"Did I ask?"

He stopped at the stop sign and put his arm along the back of the seat, grazing Maddy's bare shoulders.

The pink sundress had a row of tiny buttons between her breasts. He wondered how many. "I don't usually break my promises." *Except where you're concerned.*

"I didn't mind," she answered.

He let out his breath. "I'll bring you back here," he promised.

"I'll be gone by that weekend," she said.

"No," he stated, pulling the brim of his hat forward to shade his eyes against the bright morning sun. "No," he repeated. "You won't."

7

"STUDY TIME," Maddy announced, watching Jenna float around the pool on a bright blue air mattress. "You're going to burn," she cautioned. "Come on in the shade and let's see your book report. Where is it?"

Jenna took her time paddling over to the side of the pool where Maddy sat at the table, under the umbrella. She rested her chin on her hands and eyed her tutor. "In my room. It's not finished yet."

Maddy didn't try to hide her impatience. "You've had all week, Jen. You were supposed to let me go over it today."

Jenna shrugged. "Tomorrow, I promise."

"No way." Maddy pointed to the ladder. "Get out of the pool, grab your towel and get over here. You have some work to do."

Jenna grinned. "You mean, *we* have some work to do."

"Not me, honey. I'm not the one flunking elementary school."

Jenna did as she was told and approached the table. "I'm not flunking, and no one cares, anyway."

"Your father cares." The girl looked skeptical, so Maddy added, "Why else would he want to hire me to help you with your schoolwork? You want to get me fired?"

"Dad wouldn't do that."

Maddy shrugged, as if to say *Who knows?* "He agreed to the pool party. Now you have to do your part and write a good report."

Jenna sighed dramatically and headed toward the house. "I'll get it." When she returned she had several worn paperbacks and the hardcover edition of *Desert Stars.* "I like this book," she said. "It's sorta boring in some places but it's mostly good."

"Your report is on *The Pinball Kids,* right?"

"Yeah. That was a pretty good book." She handed Maddy a sheet of lined paper. Maddy scanned the two paragraphs and handed it back to her.

"And you have a pretty good start. Sit down and finish it."

"I'd rather read Louis Grey."

She handed her a pen. "So would I. Get busy, so we can tell your father you're making progress."

Maddy leaned back in the redwood chair, content to sit in the shade and watch the sparkling water of the pool. It was quiet on this side of the sprawling ranch house. Flowers lined the cement walkways skirting the pool, and the foothills ranged beyond. The cloudless pale blue sky went on forever.

She told herself she couldn't stay. Wouldn't stay. No matter how many times Stuart took her in his arms. Of course, they'd pretended it hadn't happened. They'd spent the rest of the morning touring the museum, with its quilt display, chuckwagon and Native American artifacts. They'd bought fishing licenses, and when they'd returned to the ranch, Stuart had packed thick sandwiches and driven off in his truck, mumbling something about checking the north range.

She'd talked to the principal's secretary, and Jenna's teacher from last year had called back just a little while ago and discussed the curriculum, listing exactly what Jenna needed to accomplish. Maddy had felt positively maternal, which was a strange and exhilarating feeling.

The Land Of Poco Tiempo, a sign had read. And it was strange, after the hustle-bustle style of New England, to be in a place where time slowed down to a crawl, and everyone operated in that style.

If it didn't get done today, it would be done tomorrow. Unfortunately, Jenna had the same attitude about her book reports. There was always tomorrow.

Maddy reached over and picked up *Desert Stars*. No matter how many times she'd read it, she could always lose herself in the story again. The beautiful heiress and the proud cowboy, the Mexican revolution, the crusty foreman and the majestic horse that galloped faster than the wind…a story of love and adventure.

It was the story that had brought her here, to this state. And yet nothing had worked out as she had planned.

Nonetheless, here she sat on a ranch at the base of the Peloncillos, cooking for the old foreman and kissing the rancher while sitting in the front of his truck. And this wasn't an adventure? Even old Louis Grey himself would have trouble believing *that* tale.

HE WAS GLAD HE HADN'T had to make a lot of excuses. He strode down a side street in Deming and wished he was anywhere else on earth. Kissing Maddy this morning seemed very far away. And here he was in Deming, for the second time today. If he spent any more time away from the ranch, he'd be forced to hire a foreman. He depended on Mac and Tom too much now.

"I wish I could look in a crystal ball and predict the

future," John said, looking very much the high-priced lawyer in his three-piece suit and snakeskin boots.

"So do I." Stuart ran his hand through his hair and wished he was anywhere else but in John Castelana's subdued, air-conditioned office.

"They're going to say you don't spend enough time with the child, that you can't possibly run a ranch the size of the Triple J and fulfill your responsibilities as a parent."

"I'm going to hire some more help." He didn't want another foreman, not after what had happened two years ago. Except now there was no Mrs. Anderson to sleep with the hired help whenever she was bored and lonely. Even so, every time he thought about hiring someone to help him, the notion stuck in his craw.

"Let me be clear about this." John leaned forward, his dark gaze holding Stuart's. "They want a fight. They want Jenna, and they're going to try every trick in the book to see that they get her. Didn't Connie leave a substantial trust fund to the child?"

"Yes, but I don't have anything to do with it. The trustees at the bank manage it."

"Good. What about the housekeeper? How is that working out?"

"I found one, at least temporarily," he answered, remembering the soft feel of Maddy's lips on his. "She's helping Jenna with her schoolwork, too, so she shouldn't have to repeat a grade."

"That one hurt," John admitted. "Low grades make it look as if no one cares."

Why in hell did everyone keep saying that? "I care," he managed to say. "Jenna knows that."

"Why is the housekeeper temporary? I want to make sure you have a housekeeper in place when we go for the hearing. And be prepared, because the judge may ask Jenna what *she* wants."

"When will that be?"

"I just found out. August twentieth. That's a Friday, at ten. We want to make sure nothing goes wrong. I have the school psychologists' reports—they're in our favor. But, Stuart, there's no way in hell to tell which side the judge will come down on. It would be different if there was a *Mrs.* Anderson."

The same old "woman's touch" thing again. "I can't come up with a mother for Jenna within the next five weeks. That's ridiculous."

"I didn't expect you to get married, but you're a very eligible bachelor. It wouldn't have surprised me if you had plans to remarry sometime in the future."

"I don't."

John stood and held out his hand. "Then that's it. I'll keep you posted if anything else comes up."

Stuart took the man's hand and thanked him. It was a long drive home, and even the slow climb through the foothills of the Peloncillos did little to distract him from the prospect of a custody hearing. Connie, never a candidate for Mother of the Year, would turn over in her grave at the thought of her parents raising Jenna. She'd finally consented to let Stuart start the adoption process. After he'd made the appointment, Connie had driven her car into a ditch at one hundred and ten miles an hour.

He'd been able to prevent Jenna from knowing about the hearing. The poor kid had had enough to deal with, and he'd hoped it could be settled without Connie's parents having their day in court. Now it looked like Jenna would have to decide where she wanted to live, and the judge would decide what was best for her.

There was only one thing he was certain of, and that was that Madeleine Harmon needed to stay on the Triple J, at least until the end of August. He would do whatever it took to make her change her mind. Jenna's future depended on it.

"I PROMISED YOU A sunset." Stuart stood in the kitchen doorway and held out his hand. "If you stay back here doing dishes you'll miss the beginning."

"But—"

"Don't argue, Maddy. Just come with me."

"All right, but—"

"Come," he interrupted. She wiped her wet hands on a checked dish towel and ignored his outstretched hand. She didn't think it was a good idea to stroll through the house holding hands with her boss. He put his hand on her back and propelled her through the living room and out the front door. She didn't have a chance to tell him there was a pineapple cake baking in the oven for dessert later. She hoped she'd hear the buzzer from the porch.

"Where is everyone?"

"Jenna is off somewhere reading and Mac is bossing the boys around in the bunkhouse." He motioned her toward a wide wooden rocking chair.

She sat down, grateful to get off her feet. Dinner had turned out to be more complicated than she'd planned. Especially since she'd had her mind on other things than food. "I thought that was your job."

He sat beside her and stretched his long legs to the porch railing. "We take turns. I hired three extra hands this week. They arrived today, expecting to go to work."

She scooted her rocker forward so she could hook her ankles on the top rail, imitating what Stuart accomplished so casually. She wore her denim shorts and once-white sneakers, which didn't project quite the same image as Stuart's jeans and familiar scuffed boots. The man practically oozed cowboy sex appeal. He could have posed for any advertisement, appeared in any commercial, with "rugged" as his middle name.

"Did I step in something?"

"What?"

"You're staring at my boots."

"Well, they're, uh, so *authentic*."

He frowned. "I guess I could buy a new pair."

"I like your boots. I didn't mean to insult you."

His surprising smile flashed toward her. "You didn't." He pointed over the railing across the wide valley below. "Watch your sunset, Maddy."

She did. She gazed across the valley as the sun blazed lower, finally disappearing below the horizon and leaving fiery red streaks behind. The sky darkened slowly, with dramatic color changes from yellow to gray, followed by the promise of twinkling stars.

"That was beautiful."

"I'm glad I took the time," he admitted. "Mac usually does, but I'd forgotten how beautiful a sunset can be."

"I'll never forget it," she promised, and she knew she wouldn't. A hopeless romantic, watching Western sunsets and blinking back tears.

"Mrs. Abernathy called and said she was still taking care of her grandchildren. Not one other person who has answered the ad—and there haven't been that many—has been suitable," Stuart said after a long comfortable silence. He cleared his throat and continued, "I'm a desperate man, Maddy. Name your price."

"There's no 'price.' It's not a question of money," she answered quietly, not daring to look at him. How could she tell him she didn't want to be needed by anyone, that she wanted an adventure, that this was the first time in years she had been totally free? That if she stayed, she risked falling in love with this place and never wanting to leave?

"Then tell me what it is."

"I have," she replied, hoping to convince him. "I'm on vacation. My grandfather left me money to travel, and that's what I'm going to do."

There was a long silence. "I'm not asking you to stay forever," he said finally. "Just until September, when Jenna will be settled in school."

"September?"

"Seven weeks. Same salary, same responsibilities."

"I'm not a housekeeper." Maybe if she kept repeating it she'd believe it herself. *I am not a housekeeper.* She might not be a housekeeper by profession, but she'd never been happier. What on earth did that say about her? She was a sucker for being needed, that's what it said.

"I'll pay you extra to do the books, too," Stuart offered. "The last foreman put everything on computer. It was supposed to make things easier but I never quite got the hang of it."

"It's easy," she said. "I'll teach you."

"You'll stay?"

She turned toward him. How could she leave now, when she was just starting to discover horses and sunsets and a handsome rancher's kisses? "Well, I guess there are a few Western fantasies I haven't fulfilled yet."

"Such as?"

Her cheeks grew warm, but she pretended not to notice the light in his blue eyes. "Fishing," she declared. "And roping a calf. And camping out."

He took her hand in his callused one and touched her index finger. "Nothing else?"

"I can't think of anything else right now."

"I can," he muttered, pulling her toward him.

"Buzzer!" Jenna yelled. "Maddy!"

"Coming!" she called to Jenna. "That's the cake." Maddy pulled her hand away from Stuart's. "I don't want it to burn."

"Are you going to stay?"

She stood and pushed the rocker back. "I guess I am. Until September."

He nodded, relief apparent in his face. "I'll make it worth it to you, Maddy."

She turned toward the door. She'd wanted adventure, and she'd gotten a lot more than she'd bargained for.

Later that evening, she sat outside by the pool, as had become a nightly tradition. Only this time Stuart didn't join her, as he had twice before. There were no salty margaritas, or stolen kisses.

She told herself she wasn't disappointed.

If she was going to stay, and she'd said she would, then she would have to be very, very careful. It would be too easy to get caught up in this life, in the slow New Mexico dream. Falling in love with the silent rancher would only bring heartache, and she'd already had her share, thank you very much. He was a loner, that was obvious. And he didn't seem to have recovered from his wife's death, either. There was a bleak look that came into his eyes when Jenna mentioned her mother.

The man wasn't looking for a woman in his life—except in the housekeeper capacity. And she wasn't looking for a husband. And she wouldn't pick one so darn quiet and serious, either.

She dipped her feet in the water and made small whirlpools by wiggling her ankles. There shouldn't be any more kisses, either. Making love with Stuart Anderson would only complicate life here on the Triple J.

When she took a lover, she wanted it to mean something more than two people giving in to a raging case of lust. And lust, she assured herself, was all that could be between herself and the silent rancher.

"IT'S YOUR TURN."

She handed him the tray of plastic glasses filled with lemonade. "No way. You're the father."

"This party was your idea."

"She's your daughter."

"It's your party."

Maddy reached up and tightened her ponytail. Outside the kitchen windows, seven screeching girls splashed in the pool. "I'm getting a headache."

"Open the door for me," he said, giving up the argument. He and Maddy had taken turns supervising the girls for the past two hours. It had seemed like fifty. "How much longer?"

She held the door open while he passed through. "Two hours, I think. Do you think it will go by fast?"

"For them or for you?"

She shut the door and watched him weave past three giggling girls and set the drinks under the umbrella on the table. The tacos were almost ready. It would be a fix-it-yourself lunch, very appropriate for poolside entertaining. She'd read all about poolside entertaining in *Sunset* magazine.

The party looked like a success. Jenna had been a nervous wreck at first, but after two of her guests had arrived she hadn't stopped smiling. Jenna had introduced Maddy as a guest from "back east," which appeared to impress the heck out of every kid. Someone asked her if she'd ever been mugged, so she'd explained she wasn't from New York City.

Mac and Homer entered the kitchen, took one look at the scene by the pool and turned around to leave.

"Not so fast," Maddy called. "Do you want any of these snacks?" She gestured toward the bowls of chips and pretzels on the kitchen table. Homer sniffed the air and left the kitchen without a backward glance.

Mac stopped. "I can eat in here?"

"Sure. Have a seat."

"I'd rather have a beer."

"Me, too."

"Good idea," Stuart said, stepping into the kitchen.

"We can't."

He went to the refrigerator and pulled out three frosty cans. "Why not?"

"I don't think proper Western hostesses slug down Bud Light when they should be chopping tomatoes or grating cheese or saving children from drowning."

"Suit yourself, but a lot of New Mexico parties include beer. For adults."

He had the damnedest way of tempting her to do things she'd never normally think of doing. "Well, all right. Maybe just one wouldn't hurt."

Stuart popped the top and handed it to her. "Jenna's having a ball. You were right, she does need friends."

"Someone should be out there supervising."

Mac shook his head. "Don't look at me. I never did like bein' 'round more than one woman at a time."

Stuart moved to the window. "I can stand here and count heads. Besides, I don't think there's anyone in the water right now."

Mac went over to stand beside him. "They've rustled up to the grub."

"Good. That's what they're supposed to be doing."

Mac turned to Maddy. "I hear you're stayin' on here for a while."

"Yep. Until fall."

"What'd this boy do to make you change your mind?"

Stuart growled at him. "Mind your own business, old man."

Mac put on an innocent expression. "Just thought I'd ask, is all. I knew it wasn't cuz of your legendary charm."

Maddy smiled. If the man only knew. "I don't mind working on a ranch for a few more weeks. I came out here to have adventures, so I guess this is the real thing."

"I s'pose," the old man drawled, but he didn't look convinced. "I guess everybody has a diff'rent idea what adventures are."

"Maddy wants to go camping. And fishing."

"And I want to learn how to rope something."

"You can practice on the fence posts," Stuart offered.

"All right." She took another cautious sip of beer and finished chopping tomatoes. Stuart wandered over and stood dangerously close. "Does that mean you're going to teach me?"

"I suppose I'll have to. You need help with anything?"

My blood pressure, she wanted to say. *Don't stand so close.* "No, thanks," she told him. "Watch the knife."

He took a step backward. "I always believe a woman when she says that."

Mac opened the door. "Is there bean dip out there?"

"Yes."

Maddy turned to watch as Mac went outside and gingerly approached the table full of snacks. Stuart chuckled. "Mac had to see what was going on."

She looked up to see him smiling down at her. "The two of you seem pretty pleased with yourselves."

He shrugged. "Why not? We've talked you into staying. Mac gets more pineapple cake and I have the right woman for Jenna."

"And I get to ride and rope and camp and—"

He stopped her words with a quick, hard kiss on her parted lips.

"Don't." She tried to protest, but the feel of his lips on hers made her forget all her resolutions to stop kissing her boss.

He lifted his head and grinned. "Couldn't resist. You looked so eager."

"I was just listing my—"

"We'll start tomorrow."

"Start what?"

"Roping." He winked at her. "I always keep my word."

"Do I get my own rope?"

"Sure."

"I saw the movie *City Slickers*. Did you?" He nodded his head, so she continued. "Remember the part where Billy Crystal had to learn how to rope a steer?"

"Yes."

"Is it as hard as it looks?"

"Harder."

"Oh."

"Until you get the hang of it." He patted her on the back, wishing he could take her into his arms again. "You'll be fine. A regular Annie Oakley."

"She shot guns."

"I'm *not* going to teach you how to do that," he sputtered.

She handed him the pottery bowl filled with chopped tomatoes. "I didn't ask."

"What's this for?"

"The taco buffet."

"Sounds fancy."

"It's worth it. I want this to be the best party Jenna ever had."

"I think it is already," he replied. "She looks pretty happy."

"She needs girlfriends. She can't just sit on this ranch all the time by herself, reading those gory mysteries and missing her mother."

"She didn't have much of a mother to miss." There was a bitterness in his voice that surprised her.

"I thought they were close."

He shook his head. "Not really. Connie put on a good front, but her number-one concern was herself. Everyone else got in line."

"But Jenna would still miss her, Stuart. Even if she wasn't the perfect mother."

He shook his head. "Perfect mother?" he repeated. "Not even close."

Maddy turned her brown eyes on him. "Then she wasn't the perfect wife, either?"

"There's no such thing," he said, smiling ruefully. "I learned that the hard way."

"You didn't say we were going to do this at six o'clock in the morning."

"It's the best time." He didn't tell her it was because he'd have no interruptions from Jenna and Mac, or any of the others, for that matter. The boys had been up since five, and on their way to various chores. He'd sent the last group out five minutes before. Mac would still be in bed or was busy fixing himself a quiet breakfast in the bunkhouse.

Stuart had Maddy all to himself, and he didn't stop to examine why he was so pleased with that fact. The morning air was cool, and he watched her shiver and rub her arms, despite the long-sleeved denim shirt and pink T-shirt she wore. She had on her jeans and boots and looked like any ranch wife getting ready to start the day. Except she wasn't anybody's wife, and she was new at all of this. The glimmer of excitement in her eyes gave her away.

"Here," he said, handing her a coiled length of rope. "I put a knot in it, like this." He demonstrated with agile fingers. "Easy, right?"

She nodded. "Right."

"Now," he said, stepping back and pulling a loop through the end of the rope. "This is the motion." The rope moved into a seemingly effortless spiral. "It's all in the wrist." He motioned for her to take the end and keep up the action.

Maddy took the end and attempted to keep the loop spinning, but it didn't last more than a few seconds.

"Try again," he said, and put his hand over hers. They both grasped the rope and he guided her hand into the right movement. When she faltered he was there to guide her hand, forcing the loop in a horizontal spin. "There, you're getting the hang of it."

"I *love* this," she breathed. "I wish—"

She faltered, and his hand tightened around hers. "Wish what, Maddy?"

"I wish I'd practiced."

The rope fell into a snakelike puddle on the hard-packed ground. "The idea is to be able to swing it over your head, let it go, and lasso something. Start with fence posts and work your way up to a moving target."

He strode across to the other side of the corral. "Like this." He started the loop, raised it high and let it go to settle neatly around Maddy's shoulders.

"Very funny," she began, but when she reached to tug it off, he pulled, tightening it around her upper arms, securing her elbows to her sides.

"This is how it works on calves," he murmured, pulling the rope so she had to walk toward him across the corral. "And beautiful women."

"You must do this a lot," she said, intrigued by this playful side she'd never seen before.

He pulled her close. "Not really. But come to think of it, now I have you where I want you," he whispered. "Ready for branding. Or anything."

"Ouch. That doesn't sound—"

"Oh, I wouldn't hurt you," he interjected, keeping the tension on the rope secure as he kissed her neck. Soft skin, warm skin, sweet skin under his lips as he moved higher, to taste the delicate nub of her earlobe. "I would hold you tight, like this." His fingers traced the rope where it nestled across her breasts. "You wouldn't be able to get away."

"I can't get away now," she argued.

His lips teased her cheek. "Sure you can."

It wasn't easy to protest, not when he moved his mouth to the corner of her lips and planted tiny kisses there. "You're supposed to be teaching me how to rope," she managed.

"I am. There are all sorts of advantages to learning, you see."

"I don't think I'm learning—" He captured her lips for a deep, searing kiss. A sunrise kiss, full of promise and heady with dusky aftertones of the night before. Possessive, even.

His hands grasped her shoulders and held her upright. Kissing Maddy was something Stuart figured he could definitely get used to. He wanted to make love to her, and would have, if they'd been standing anywhere but in the middle of the corral in front of the stock barn and within sight of the bunkhouse. There'd been enough interest in the "little broad from the East" as it was. The next young cowboy who called her a broad would eat his teeth for breakfast.

Make her his? Yes, definitely. Whatever that meant. He didn't want to stop kissing her, but there was always a chance someone was watching.

He reluctantly lifted his mouth from hers. When he made love to Madeleine Harmon, he wanted privacy.

8

SHE'D HAD NO IDEA roping could be so, well, erotic.

He'd released her, and she'd stepped back. Just a little.

And looked up at him. Just for a second.

She'd waited for him to say something, just a few words. But he'd removed the rope and handed it to her.

"You'll get the hang of it," he'd said after a long moment.

"I'll keep practicing," she'd answered. And instead of shaking out the rope to try again, she'd coiled it up and, heart pounding at a rapid rate, walked back to the house.

Maddy poured herself a cup of coffee in the quiet kitchen, relieved that she had the room to herself. She didn't have to hide her shaking fingers or pretend her insides weren't rioting. It had been years since she'd felt something even close to that kind of passion. She kept telling herself that Stuart's kisses shouldn't affect her the way they did—like riding a runaway horse. Is this what happened when a woman had been alone too long?

It would be too easy to fall into Stuart's arms, with or without being roped. It would be too easy to let herself make love to him, too easy to slip into a convenient summer-cowboy fantasy. Like a bad joke, she'd fallen for the first cowboy to make a move on her.

She didn't usually bring out the animal lust in men. She wasn't exactly the femme-fatale type. Taking care of an invalid grandfather didn't give a person the chance to experience an array of sexual escapades.

Forget the array. Maddy smiled to herself. *One* would have been enough.

Maddy tried not to think about making love to Stuart. She didn't want to imagine him kicking off his boots, unzipping those jeans, or flinging his cowboy hat across the bed. *Think about housekeeping,* she told herself. *Think about work.*

She drank half of her coffee. She was supposed to have the day off, but she didn't know what on earth she'd do with it. She wasn't exactly overworked as it was. She needed to make a grocery list and a shopping trip to Deming tomorrow, which meant a week's menus to plan. Then there was a review of Jenna's new book; she'd probably have to read it herself so she could help Jenna if she got stuck.

For now, she'd whip up some scrambled eggs and sausages for anyone who was interested in eating.

She'd practice roping as soon as breakfast was over and she found a small pair of work gloves. She intended to spend a large part of her day conquering the lasso. Jenna had helped her a lot with her riding, and she felt comfortable on Snake. Now, if she could only rope something. A fence post would do for a start, but something live would be even better.

Maddy started cracking eggs into a large bowl. It was almost seven-thirty, but it felt a lot later. She was certainly growing accustomed to ranch hours. She'd be taking siestas in the afternoon any day now. *The land of poco tiempo*. It was also the land of enchantment and starry skies. Kissing Stuart meant she was falling under its spell. It would be better for her peace of mind if she avoided being alone with her boss. There was only so much temptation one woman could withstand.

"I finished the book," Jenna announced, bouncing into the kitchen. She was a different girl this morning; some of the clouds were gone from her eyes, and her lips curved easily into a smile. "Just now!"

"Did you like it?" Maddy didn't have to ask what book Jenna meant. The girl had been reading *The Lights of the Desert Stars* whenever she had a spare minute.

"I *loved* it. Especially the horse."

"What did you think of the ending?"

"That was the *best* part," she said. "I was so scared he wouldn't find her, that she would die if he couldn't get to her in time."

"I think I bit my nails throughout the last fifty pages when I read it for the first time."

"Yeah. Me, too."

"I'm glad you liked it."

"I wish it could count for my summer reading." She stepped closer to the counter and wrapped her arms around Maddy in an enthusiastic hug. "Thanks for yesterday, Maddy. It was a totally awesome party, and three of the girls invited me to their house this summer. Doesn't that sound like fun?" She kept her arms around Maddy and looked up. Maddy realized that in a few short years Jenna would be as tall as she was. "I can go, can't I? Say yes, please?"

"Of course you can, if your father agrees, and I don't see why he wouldn't."

"If I agree to what?" Stuart entered the kitchen and

tipped his hat back in that familiar gesture Maddy was learning to look for.

Jenna dropped her arms quickly and stepped back, her expression guilty. "Will you let me go to a friend's house sometime? I've been invited."

"We'll see," he answered, and then saw the disappointment on Jenna's face. "Well, I guess it sounds okay to me. As long as you keep up with your reading."

Relief made her jump up and down. "Thanks!" She turned back to Maddy. "Are we going riding?"

"Maybe later. Do you want breakfast?" The girl nodded. "I'll call you when the eggs are ready."

"Great." Jenna went outside and perched on the edge of the pool.

Maddy looked over at Stuart. So much for avoiding being alone with him. It was very important, she reminded herself, to forget about that passionate kiss in the corral. He'd kissed her as if he wanted a lot more, and she'd returned the kiss as if she was saying yes to anything he asked. Was that any way for a housekeeper to behave? "Scrambled eggs all right with you?"

He looked at her as if he wasn't thinking about scrambling eggs. Those silver-blue eyes began to twinkle with mischief, and something else. "Sounds fine."

"And sausage?"

"Fine, too." He took a step toward her as if he wanted to be closer, but Maddy turned away, breaking eye contact. If she was in danger of falling in love with Stuart Anderson, then she'd better get used to pretending it wasn't happening. In fact, now was as good as any time to start.

"Give me fifteen minutes."

He went to her side and took a coffee mug from the cupboard. "I'll read the paper." He took his time pouring a cup of coffee and replaced the carafe. "Isn't this your day off?"

"I suppose so," she said, beating the eggs with a fork. "It doesn't really matter."

"You can't work seven days a week."

"I don't mind." He didn't look convinced so Maddy hurried to reassure him. "If it makes you feel any better, I'd like some extra time in town tomorrow. I'm going to need a few more clothes, and I'd like to go to the library. That is, if I can have the truck."

"There's a car stored in the big shed. I'll have one of the boys make sure it's started up for you."

"Okay."

"And don't worry about dinner tonight. We'll go out. I'll take you to Shakespeare this afternoon, and then we'll have dinner."

"We will?" Was that a family "we" or a date "we"? Guess she'd have to wait to find out. Surely he couldn't mean just the two of them.

"Sure. You could use the break."

"I'm not exactly working myself to death, but I wouldn't turn down a chance to see that ghost town, and I'd like to send some more postcards. But don't think you have to do it if you have other work to do."

"We'll leave at twelve-thirty," he declared. "No arguments." Then, almost as an afterthought, he added, "Are you taking Jenna to town with you tomorrow?"

She nodded and started placing sausages in the skillet. "If that's all right with you."

"It's fine. She prefers the car, but I try to avoid driving the damn thing."

"You don't like cars?" Maybe New Mexico men only drove trucks.

"It was Connie's. Or rather, it's the car I bought to replace the one that was totaled."

"I'm sorry."

"Don't be. I would have divorced her, if it hadn't meant losing Jenna. Connie had a different idea of what marriage should be. Different from what I thought, that's for damn sure." He leaned back against the counter and took a sip of coffee. "My foreman was with her. He was banged up pretty bad, but at least he survived." He winced. "Connie liked men. She found life here on the ranch pretty tame."

So Miss New Mexico had had an affair with her husband's foreman and in the process, killed herself on Highway 70. Which was why Stuart didn't have a wife *or* a foreman. She put her hand on his arm. "Stuart, I really am sorry."

"Well, it's over now." The bleak look left his eyes as he looked down at her. "It happened years ago," he added. "It doesn't have anything to do with today."

She turned away to poke at the sausages, which were starting to sizzle in the pan. Why didn't she believe him? Losing a wife that way would have to affect him, for a long, long time. Somehow she knew there were things he wasn't telling her, even though she was amazed he'd confided in her at all. At least it explained why Jenna acted as if she was alone; from the sound of it, she'd been on her own for years. Both the man and the child needed a lot of love.

But she was the wrong woman to give it to them. She'd be better off concentrating on rope tricks.

The rest of the morning passed slowly. Maddy served breakfast and talked to Mac about the weather and the complexities of learning to rope. Stuart disappeared, which was probably a pretty good thing except that Maddy found herself looking for him at odd moments, not knowing if she was disappointed when he wasn't there or if she was relieved that he wasn't around to create havoc with her hormones. She read Jenna's next assignment in the shade of the umbrella, and kept a watchful eye as the child swam in the pool.

When Jenna decided it was more fun to talk on the telephone than swim, Maddy went inside and fixed herself a glass of iced tea. She thought she'd have a shower and condition her hair. She'd wear the yellow sundress she'd brought for evenings and hadn't had a chance to wear.

Was it silly to be dressing up? Probably. She didn't want to think about how long it had been since she'd been on a date. Last December the young mother next door had invited her to dinner to meet her brother. The brother had drunk too much and grabbed her knee under the dining-room table. Then Sandy, her best friend since eighth grade, had fixed her up with three blind dates—all disastrous—before Maddy had finally begged for mercy and said, "Absolutely never again."

Never again had been a very long time ago.

Now she didn't know if they were going to load up all "the boys" in the trucks and head for the Burger King drive-up window or sit down at a linen-covered table. Despite all her resolutions to stay away from Stuart, Maddy couldn't help but hope for a table for two.

WAITING IN FRONT OF the porch was a big silver Lincoln Continental. "Thought you'd look too good for the truck" was all Stuart said, tossing a light-colored sport coat in the back seat of the car. He wore dark brown slacks and an ivory button-down shirt. It was open at the neck, revealing his tanned throat. He looked like a cattle baron, lean and dark, ready for action. There wasn't another cowhand in sight.

"Thanks, I think." This car was what he expected her to drive to town tomorrow? It was three times as big as her Ford Fiesta.

He opened the passenger door and gestured toward the empty seat. "Aren't you going to get in?"

She stepped off the porch and slid onto the creamy leather. "Where's Jenna?"

"She said she's been on three school field trips to Shakespeare, and besides, her 'best friend' Melissa was calling her back this afternoon."

"But she'll be alone." *We'll* be alone.

"Mac's with her. They're going to finish up the leftovers from the party and watch a movie later on. I don't know who is taking care of whom, but it seems to work out."

"They seem very attached to each other."

"She doesn't have much family."

"Not even grandparents?"

His face closed. "Oh, she has grandparents, all right."

Maddy waited for him to elaborate, but he slammed the car door shut and went around to the driver's side. Once in, he turned the key in the ignition and the motor quietly started.

"I thought you didn't like driving this car."

"I couldn't very well take you out to dinner in the old truck." His expression softened as he glanced over at her. "I like that color."

The simple compliment pleased her. "Thank you."

It was an afternoon Maddy knew she'd always remember. They were met at the gate of the town by a couple dressed in Western garb. The small buildings of Shakespeare—once called Mexican Springs—had been lovingly and authentically restored by the owners, and there was something about the bright blue sky as a backdrop that gave Maddy goose bumps. Stuart pointed out the old hotel where Billy the Kid supposedly had washed dishes. The Grant House dining room, with its dirt floors and original yucca ceilings, had seen several hangings; Maddy knew she'd never forget the eerie sight of nooses hanging from the ceiling.

She learned it had been a wild boom town, once filled with prospectors hungry for gold and anything else they could find in the nearby mountains. Every Western novel she had ever read came to life right there in Shakespeare.

"Well?" Stuart put his hand at the small of her back and guided her toward the shining car in the parking lot. "What did you think? Not disappointed, are you?"

"I loved it. I wish—" She hesitated, not wanting to sound maudlin.

"Wish what?"

"That my grandfather could have seen it all with me."

"You must miss him."

"Yes. He would have loved this country." She looked out the window at the wide, flat land as Stuart guided the car onto the highway. "It goes on forever, just like the books said."

"Jenna thinks I should start reading your Louis Grey book. What is it called?"

"*The Lights of the Desert Stars.* You can borrow it anytime you want."

He smiled. "I don't have much time for reading. But you've worked miracles with Jenna."

"Not really. She just needed someone to talk to."

"I'm not much of a talker," he admitted. "I guess you've figured that out."

"I'm getting used to it." She grinned at him. "I probably talk enough for three people, so it evens out."

He stepped on the gas, and the car leaped forward down the empty highway. "I don't mind the way you talk. At least there's a little life in the house now."

Another compliment. Stuart was certainly in an odd mood.

Miles sped by. "Are you starving?" he asked.

"Not yet."

"I thought we'd drive over to Las Cruces for dinner."

"Las Cruces? Isn't that a long way east of here?"

"About a hundred and twenty miles."

"You want to drive that far for dinner?"

"It's not that far. And besides, we have the rest of the day. The air-conditioning works, you'll see more of the country. If we're going to sightsee, we may as well go all the way."

"All right."

The two hours passed quickly. She asked him questions about the ranch, and he told her how his great-grandfather had settled at the base of the Peloncillos, and started what would become the family business.

She told herself she shouldn't enjoy being with him so much.

He told himself he should have done this sooner. He should keep her away from the ranch as long as possible. He liked having her all to himself.

It just felt right.

He tried to ignore the tightening in his groin at the thought of her thighs just inches from his. The yellow dress floated around her knees and hugged her waist, making her look like a flower just waiting to be picked. When had she changed from the mousy woman at the train station to the beauty beside him in the car? Her skin had a golden sheen now, and her hair was looser, curlier. Her mouth was more relaxed, too.

He liked that mouth. If he had to hog-tie her again to kiss her, he would. Whatever he had to do, it would damn well be worth it.

Maybe he felt this way only because he hadn't had a woman in a long time. But he knew better. There'd been a few opportunities with women after Connie died, but he'd avoided getting involved. He'd figured they all had an ulterior motive. And sexual attraction was a pretty poor barometer for judging women.

But not this woman. He wanted Maddy in a way he'd never wanted a woman before. The problem was, what was he going to do about it? He knew what he'd *like* to do about it. Make love to her and get it out of his system. If she'd let him. Something told him it wouldn't be that easy. Maddy sure had some odd notions.

"I'm taking you to the Cattle Baron Steak House." He glanced over at her and grinned. "Thought the name might suit your idea of a Western restaurant."

"It sounds perfect."

"They serve a pretty good steak."

The restaurant suited Maddy just fine. She and Stuart drank huge icy margaritas in a Western-decorated bar and, once at a small table in the corner, were served giant salads, steaks and baked potatoes. It was about as Western as she could have hoped for.

And when they'd finished, they drove off into the sunset. Maddy could have wept with delight.

"SON OF A BITCH."

Maddy ran the comb through her wet hair and wondered why Stuart was swearing. She stood wrapped in a towel, staring into her foggy bathroom mirror as Stuart swore in his new office on the other side of the door. Something obviously wasn't going well.

"Damn thing," she heard him mutter. She went back to her room and tossed on a pair of shorts and a T-shirt and padded barefoot down the hall to the other bedroom. The door was half open, and when she looked in she saw Stuart bent over a card table, frowning at a computer monitor. He was dressed in his work clothes, but it was six-thirty. Usually he was out with the boys this time of the morning.

She knocked on the door, pushing it open wide. "Stuart?"

He looked up, his mouth set in a grim line. "How in hell do these damn things work?"

Maddy figured that was as close to asking for help as he was going to get. "What are you trying to do?"

"Update these feed records. I've got cattle scattered over miles, and by fall I'll need to account for every one. Plus the quarterly tax statements. I have to pay some damn payroll tax to the IRS."

Maddy stepped closer and peered over his shoulder. The familiar program wasn't complicated, from what she could see. "Can you enter the dollar amounts in that column?"

"Not yet."

"How have you been keeping up with all this since your foreman left?"

"The old-fashioned way." He grimaced. "Pencil and paper. I dug the computer out of the closet last night and figured out how to hook it up. That's about as far as I could get."

"Do you want to learn how or do you want me to do it for you?"

"Do it for me," he replied, his expression still thunderous. "I'll learn later, when I don't feel like throwing this damn thing into the mesquite."

"Fair enough." She eyed the piles of paperwork. "Give me a brief description of what you're trying to do, one project at a time, and when I have some time later on I'll figure it out for myself."

He pushed back his chair in relief. "I knew it was my lucky day when I picked you up at the train station."

"No, you didn't." She leafed through a stack of papers. They looked like bills of sale for cattle, but she couldn't be sure. "You thought you'd been saddled with a pretty strange housekeeper, didn't you?"

He towered over her and grinned. "Well, you sure took a lot of pictures."

"I thought you were a pretty strange cowboy, you know."

He touched the bare skin of her arm and inched higher in a disturbing caress. "You smell good."

"Soap," she replied, tossing the papers back onto the card table. "I just got out of the shower."

"I heard the water running. What were you singing?"

"You heard me?"

He nodded, tugging her closer. "Sounded like something country and western to me."

Maddy thought about resisting going into his arms for a second. This was very, very dangerous. Because it felt so very, very right. "I think it was 'Mama, Don't Let Your Babies Grow Up to Be Cowboys.'"

"Willie Nelson," he murmured, bending his head close to hers. "Of course."

His breath was warm on her cheek, making it hard to concentrate on the conversation. "I heard you, too."

He kissed the corner of her mouth. "I wasn't singing."

"No, you were swearing."

"I swear when I'm frustrated." He kissed the other corner of her mouth and then looked down into her eyes. "What about you?"

She blinked. "What about me?"

"Do you swear when you're frustrated?"

"No." It was hopeless, Maddy realized, putting her arms around his neck. Maybe it was simple physical attraction, but it was powerful nonetheless. When his lips met hers, she didn't want to pull away, and she didn't want to pretend it wasn't what she wanted.

She wanted to pretend he loved her.

An overwhelming kiss, it would have knocked her to her knees if she hadn't held on to him. His lips were warm, demanding, taking what he wanted. He urged her lips apart and tasted the inside of her mouth, teasing her tongue with erotic messages. His hands slipped under her T-shirt and slid over her waist and higher, to cup lace-covered breasts.

Maddy gasped against his mouth, but still he didn't release her. He backed her against the card table, its rounded edges pressed against her bare legs.

He lifted his mouth from hers and slipped his hands down and around her waist. In a swift motion he sat down on the metal folding chair, pulling her onto his lap.

"Better," he murmured.

"Stuart," she began, but his lips took hers again. She opened her mouth willingly, ready to fall into whatever spell he cast upon her. Her arms twined around his neck and her fingers tangled in his hair.

He raised his head. "What?"

"We shouldn't—"

He stopped her words with a quick, hard kiss on her mouth, then lower, to her neck. His lips found the quickened pulse at the hollow of her throat.

Maddy shifted, suddenly conscious of her intimate position on his lap.

"You're going to hurt me doing that," he said, humor threading his voice.

She stilled, more self-conscious than ever. She felt like some saloon girl in the movies, perched on the cowboy's lap while he called for another round of whiskey. All she needed was black net stockings and a red satin dress to complete the picture. Madeleine Harmon, the cowboys' sweetheart. "I should go fix breakfast," she tried, although she made no move to leave.

"Not hungry," he told her, his hands moving to caress her breasts. "Are you?"

"Starving," she lied, silently cursing the weakness that coursed through her as he touched her.

"Liar."

She slid off his lap and stood facing him. "This isn't a very good idea."

"That's where you're wrong, sweetheart," he said, surprising her by taking her hand and bringing it to his lips in an old-fashioned gesture.

She melted. She just couldn't help it. "It's not you, it's me."

He frowned, releasing her hand. "There's nothing the matter with you."

She quickly fastened her bra and tugged her shirt down. "I didn't say there was anything *wrong*. I just meant that I don't..."

"Don't what?"

"Don't go around sitting on laps and taking off my underwear."

"I didn't think you did."

"How would you know?" She smoothed her shirt. "You picked me up at a train station a couple of weeks ago and now here I am sitting on your lap and we almost knocked the computer off the table."

"Good riddance."

She didn't answer his grin. "You don't know what kind of woman I am."

"I know, all right."

She looked at him and wished she could go back into his arms. There was something safe there, even though the feelings he aroused inside her were anything but tame.

He took her hand again and tugged her closer to stand between his legs. "It's called physical attraction, Maddy. Chemistry."

"But—"

"Wait," he interjected, cutting off her protest. "I don't go around seducing women. Hell, I don't even date any."

"Why not?"

He shook his head. "After being married to Connie, living alone is like a vacation. Guess I've been too much of a coward to put myself through that again." He looked up at her. "And I still am."

She wanted to go back into his arms, experience

more of the pleasure she found there. She'd like to strip off all her clothes and feel Stuart's hard body on top of hers, inside her, around her.

But she couldn't. If she could somehow figure out how to avoid his realizing she was still a virgin, then she would be tempted, but that was impossible. It was bad enough to have to learn how to ride and rope and fish, embarrassing to know nothing about being a cowgirl. But this was the most intimate knowledge of all. Who'd believe a twenty-eight-year-old virgin?

"I think I'd better go make breakfast," she said, backing out of the room.

She hurried down the hall and turned the kitchen lights on before she was tempted to turn around and run back to the cowboy swearing in the bedroom. Curiosity wasn't the best reason to make love to Stuart. Falling in love with him was the best reason not to.

9

IT WAS EASY TO AVOID him. Easier than she would have thought possible. Maybe, Maddy mused, he wanted to avoid her, too.

That thought didn't make her happy.

She wasn't used to passion. Wasn't comfortable with it, didn't know how to deal with the feelings. And she wanted more of it, however it made her feel.

She'd gone over and over Monday morning's kiss. Kisses. He'd made it clear he wanted her. Also made it clear he wasn't going to marry again. Fair enough. Although she dreamed of marriage and a family someday, this wasn't a good time for commitments. This was the summer for freedom and adventure.

Did "adventure" mean making love with Stuart Anderson?

"WELL, YOU LADIES'D have to git up early," Mac drawled. "Would you pass that applesauce over here, honey?"

Jenna lifted the bowl and handed it to him. "I can get up early," she insisted. "I do it all the time."

"Me, too," Maddy agreed, spearing a piece of steak. She'd discovered the charcoal grill under a tarp by the pool and had cleaned it up in time for tonight's dinner.

"And no complainin'," he warned, spooning the fruit onto his plate. "I hate complainin' women."

Maddy smiled. "We won't complain."

He shook his head. "I hope you won't take this the wrong way, Miss Maddy, but I find that mighty hard to believe. Nothing personal, though."

"That's okay, Mac." Maddy winked at Jenna, who grinned back. "We'll just have to prove it to you."

The front door banged shut and Stuart strode into the house, pausing at the dining-room table.

"Sorry I'm late," he muttered. "It's been one thing after another."

Mac looked up. "Did you see Tim? He called the bunkhouse twice today. You've got a sick horse."

Stuart took off his hat. "Yeah. It's all straightened out." He turned to Maddy. "I'll go wash up."

"I kept your steak warm."

"Thanks."

When he returned his face was ruddy, as if he'd scrubbed over sunburned cheekbones. He wore a fresh shirt, with sleeves rolled up past the wrists. He sat down, a cold bottle of beer in his hand, as Maddy rose and took his empty plate.

"Finish your dinner," he said. "You don't have to wait on me."

She took his plate anyway. "I'm finished," she said. "And this is part of my job."

He glared at her. "You're not a servant, for heaven's sake."

She didn't know why she felt like arguing with him. Maybe it was because, except for mealtimes, she hadn't seen him in days. He'd missed some meals, too. And those he ate were mostly in silence.

"We're going fishing," Jenna announced, shooting her father a worried glance. "Want to come?"

Stuart watched Maddy leave the room. "You finally talked him into it, Maddy?" he called after her.

"Yes!"

He was still chuckling when she returned, bringing his plate heaped with steak and an oversize baked potato. She put it in front of him with great ceremony, then returned to her place at the table.

Mac shook his head. "They've been talking 'bout it all week. Now it's Friday and I've jest given up."

Stuart took a swallow of beer, looking as if he was trying not to laugh. "How are you going to teach both of them at once? Have you thought of that?"

"I dunno." The old man's face brightened. "You're goin' to go with me," he declared, pleased with himself. "Perfect solution to my problem."

Stuart looked over at Maddy. She couldn't figure out what his expression meant. His blue eyes began to twinkle. "All right," he said. "It takes a wise man to admit he needs help."

Maddy wondered if he was still talking about fishing.

SHE WAS GOING TO CATCH a fish if it killed her. She had her camera ready for the big event, and intended to have her picture taken holding her fish. She would have the photo enlarged, framed and mounted on the living-room wall. "Oh, yes," she would say casually to guests who asked. "That was from my vacation in New Mexico last year."

And then, if they begged her, she'd push back the couch and do a few rope tricks.

But first she had to master the fine art of casting. That meant flicking the pole and releasing the line without getting anything hung up in trees, rocks or logs.

It was harder than it looked.

Especially with Stuart standing beside her on the bank of the small stream. They'd driven up into the Coronado National Forest, south of the ranch and, according to Mac, close to the Mexican border. Mac and Jenna had found a spot downstream, leaving Maddy and Stuart alone with their fishing poles and gear and a promise to meet them for an early lunch in three hours.

They walked in the opposite direction along the bank of the stream for a while, until Stuart determined that he'd found a good spot for trout. Once that was decided, Maddy set the tackle box down on the rocky ground and watched Stuart fix the fishing poles.

That was a show in itself. He silently concentrated on attaching the little feathered flies to the lines, then instructed Maddy in the fine art of casting. She thought it similar to roping, and tried to imitate Stuart's easy whipping motion. It wasn't easy, but she didn't really expect it to be.

"Think we'll catch anything?"

Stuart reeled in his line. "Sure."

"This must be a good spot."

He shrugged. "Keep thinking like that. Optimism is the first requirement for a fisherman."

"So you think we'll catch a lot of fish?"

"Of course. The second requirement is silence. You don't want to scare them away."

No, she didn't want to scare off the fish whose picture would decorate her grandfather's living room, so Maddy tried to be quiet. And she succeeded, until her line caught on the branch of a log partially submerged in the rocky stream.

"Stuart," she whispered. "I think I have a problem."

He looked up and recognized her problem. "Yeah. Either you've caught a fish or your line's hung up."

"The line's hung up."

He set down his pole, took hers and tugged. "Hung up, all right." He handed the pole back to her. "Set it down," he told her, as he sat down on the rocky bank. He started to pull off his boots.

"What are you doing?"

"Going in."

"I'm sorry you have to go to all the trouble."

He looked up at her, surprised. "It's no problem, Maddy. It's part of fishing."

"Well, in that case shouldn't I go in and untangle it myself?"

He stood and slipped off his watch. "That's not necessary."

"I want to." She kicked off her sneakers, then leaned over to strip off her socks.

"Women," he muttered, wading into the water. Maddy tugged off her jeans, glad she'd worn her bathing suit under her clothes. Stuart turned around, obviously about to give her another order. "What the hell are you doing? Stay on the shore, Maddy. And stop taking your clothes off."

"I don't want to get my jeans wet. I have my bathing suit on."

"Oh." He grinned. "I thought you were trying to tell me something."

She started to laugh. "No."

He pretended to act disappointed. "Then we're just fishing?"

"Yep." She started wading in after him, her shirt brushing the tops of her thighs. The rocks were rounded, the bottom sandy. She went deeper, almost to her thighs, before she reached the log.

"Watch out," he warned. "The bottom could drop off into a hole and you'd be in over your head."

"Okay."

"Hold the log steady. I think I've almost got it."

The current was stronger than she'd imagined, but she managed to get a grip on the log while Stuart fiddled with the fishing line.

"Got it!" He held up the end of the line, its fly slightly mangled.

She let go of the log and cheered. It bounced against her thighs and knocked her off-balance. Stuart automatically stuck out his hand to help her. As his fingers grasped hers, she slipped on the rocky bottom and fell backward, taking her fishing instructor with her.

The water wasn't cold, but it certainly surprised her to be splashing around in it. Stuart got up and tugged her to her feet. "So much for the fish," he muttered, smoothing his hair out of his eyes.

Maddy regained her balance and started laughing. Stuart didn't look like the stern rancher now. His shirt was plastered to his very wide chest, and his jeans hugged his hips. Water dripped down his forehead. "Sorry," she tried to say, but her giggles overcame her apology.

"Aw, hell," he muttered, taking two strides to her. He put his hands on her shoulders and kissed her, hard. Water streamed down their faces, mingling with their lips.

It was exactly what she wanted.

Maddy felt the imprint of his fingers warming her skin through the wet fabric of her shirt. The water tickled her knees as she leaned into Stuart's kiss, wanting more than simply his mouth tasting her mouth, her tongue tangling with his. She reached for his waist, feeling the smooth denim under her palms, the water dripping from his shirt.

"I've been trying to avoid this," he said, lifting his head to look down into her eyes.

"Me, too," she confessed, still holding on to his waist.

He frowned. "I'm not going to apologize for wanting you."

"Me neither," she whispered.

Stuart's expression softened. "I guess we're both through fighting it."

She looked up into his eyes, wondering if he could tell she had fallen in love with him. Fighting it had done no good at all. "How hard were you fighting?"

He smiled. "Took everything I had."

At least she knew she wasn't the only one. "Really?"

"Really." He took a deep breath. "I won't hurt you, Maddy."

She wished she could believe him, but even through the passionate haze of wanting him, she knew he could promise no such thing. "Don't make promises like that," she cautioned.

He shook his head, lowering his lips to her neck, and skimmed his hands along the swell of her breasts. "I would never hurt you," he promised once again. "But if you want me to stop, I will."

"No," Maddy decided, suddenly certain that making love with Stuart was the only choice she had right now, the only choice she wanted to make.

"Come on," he said, guiding her toward the riverbank. She almost lost her balance once more, when her foot met a slippery rock, but Stuart's strong arms saved her from falling face forward into the water. He stopped on the bank and kissed her again, his lips seeking hers with a possessive intensity that made her knees go weak.

"What about Jenna and Mac?" she managed to say when he released her and began to unbutton his shirt.

"We're not supposed to meet them for hours yet." He peeled off his wet shirt and hung it on a tree branch to dry. "Besides, they have the food. They won't come looking for us."

"But—"

He turned to smile at her, and she longed to smooth her palms along his muscled chest. She wondered what the furred chest hair would feel like against her lips. "We're alone," he assured her. "And we're getting out of our wet clothes because we fell in the water."

She couldn't help smiling back at him, despite the nervous flutters in the pit of her stomach. She tugged her T-shirt over her head and Stuart took it and spread it in the shady overhang made by the trees.

"Come here," he said, and she realized he'd used his shirt as a curtain to protect their privacy. He spread out the old blanket he'd insisted she'd need on this trip because she'd find fishing boring and would want to read instead.

But fishing—and anything else they were doing—was anything but boring. Trees arched around them on three sides, and their shirts hung like a private door on the fourth. If this was what falling in love was all about, she wished she'd admitted it sooner. When Stuart looked at her, the longing and passion visible in his eyes, she wondered how she'd made it through the week without noticing that expression on his face.

Making love to this man was inevitable. There was a certain rightness about it that she'd never known before.

There was something else she'd never known before, and she had to tell him. "Stuart, you remember that I didn't know how to ride very well?"

"Yes," he murmured, slipping one strap off her shoulder and kissing the bare skin. "You're a lot better now," he told her. "And you hardly ever shout 'yippee' anymore."

"Thank you. And remember how you had to teach me how to rope?"

"Yeah," he answered, slipping off the other strap. "I hate to tell you, Maddy, but I don't think you have a natural aptitude for rope tricks." He took one index finger and slid it along the edge of her bodice, tugging it lower to reveal the upper swell of her breasts. He kissed each soft mound before moving the top down, revealing her breasts, and holding them in his hands. "Beautiful," he said, stroking them to respond.

Heat coursed through her, and she moaned softly. "Stuart, I'm trying to tell you something. Please—" Her breath caught in her throat as his lips nuzzled one pink nipple, then the other. "Stuart, what I'm trying to tell you is that you have to teach me this, too," she finally managed to say.

"Teach you what, sweetheart?" He looked into her eyes.

"This," she replied. "I've never made love to anyone before."

It took a second to sink in. She wanted to close her eyes so she wouldn't see his reaction, but she didn't. Would he be disgusted or pleased? She'd read somewhere that most men didn't want the responsibility of a woman's first time. Would Stuart reject her, or would he want her more than ever?

"All right," he said, his gaze searching hers. "We'll go slow, as long as you're sure."

She nodded, relieved that he hadn't walked away. "I'm sure."

"Your fiancé didn't—"

She shook her head. "No."

"And you've never—"

"No."

"You're sure I'm the man you—"

Oh, she wanted him, all right. She put her finger against his lips. Total honesty was all she could manage right now, standing half naked under the shady trees. "I can't imagine wanting anyone more than I want you," she told him. Then, uncertain whether or not he'd changed his mind, she added, "If you don't mind."

"*Mind?*" He ran his fingers along her breasts, cupping them with reverent hands. "Maddy, for God's sake, why would I mind making love to you?"

Heat flooded her body again, settling in intimate places. "I don't have any idea," she said, reaching for him. His chest hair was crinkly under her touch, and the flat nipples oddly intriguing beneath her fingertips. She didn't feel the least bit shy; after all, she'd thought about making love to Stuart before. Now it was a reality, and the reality was better than any of the daydreams had been.

He was hers, at least for this present moment, and his skin was under her hands and his fingers caressed her, and when he peeled her wet bathing suit past her hips, she helped him, stepping out of the fabric and leaving it on the faded blue blanket.

He unfastened his jeans and tossed them aside, to be followed by the rest of his clothing, until they stood naked before each other. Strangely she felt no embarrassment. Her body, now golden from the New Mexico sun, was stronger from all the riding and exercise. She didn't feel bony or awkward any longer.

Stuart was beautifully formed, she realized, from his square shoulders and his chest, paler than his muscled arms, to the narrow tapering of his waist; then lower, to his rigid shaft and strong thighs.

He kissed her again, with a greater sense of possession, and Maddy answered him with her own need, a need that was growing stronger with each passing second. Somewhere overhead a bird trilled, and the gurgle of the stream covering the rocks was the only answering sound. Other than her breathing, which had grown ragged, there was little sound to distract them. Wanting him had been torture; having him would be heaven.

He released her, tugging her down to the blanket.

"We'll take it slow," he said, leaning over her.

She'd take it any way she could get it, Maddy thought. After years of reading love scenes, she was finally going to experience the real thing. "All right."

His lips tickled her neck, and lower, to tease the tip of each breast. He lay beside her, propping himself on his elbow and leaving one arm free to touch and explore her waiting body. "You have skin like silk," he said, running his palm from her breast to her hipbone, and lower, to her flat abdomen.

"Don't I get to touch you?"

He shook his head. "Not yet." His finger dipped lower. "It's my turn to touch here." He smoothed his palm over her mound. "And here." He parted her with gentle fingers, leaving Maddy to wonder if she'd die from the exquisite, torturous sensations building within her. "And here," he groaned, dipping into the creamy center of her.

Maddy gasped, and Stuart covered her mouth with his. His tongue stroked her, as his fingers opened her. She widened, wanting more.

"Just a minute, sweetheart," he said, withdrawing from her. He returned to the blanket and Maddy moved to her side to look at him. "Protection," he said, and she saw that he'd come prepared. He sensed the unspoken question in her eyes. "Ranch policy," he explained. "No single hand goes anywhere without a condom in his pocket. Not even the boss."

"I'm glad." She couldn't believe she was talking about this, but it made her feel she was with a man who cared enough to protect them both. "I should have thought about that sooner."

He kissed her. "You don't have to worry," he assured her. "I promised you I wouldn't hurt you, didn't I?" He shifted his body closer to hers. "Put your leg over my hip," he said. He held her bottom with one large hand, fitting himself against her.

The position gave him full access to her mouth, and he took her mouth with his, breathing her breath, feeling her sigh as he pressed himself into her. Her tight warmth surrounded him, and he lifted his lips to look into her eyes. "This might hurt," he warned.

"I don't think so." And her smile almost undid him. "You feel wonderful inside me," she murmured, and he felt himself swell larger than he would have imagined.

But he didn't want to hurt her, although he didn't know how much more he could take. He gripped her bottom again, holding her tightly against him while he thrust forward. The barrier was minimal, the sliding into Maddy's welcoming body accompanied by a wave of pleasure so intense he had to clench his jaw to keep from crying out.

Her arms tightened around him, and he slowed, determined to bring her pleasure. And he did, after long, long moments under the cottonwood trees by the banks of the stream in the Coronado forest.

He felt her tighten around him, felt the tiny tremors rock her body, and he could take no more. He stroked her through the shattering climax and joined her, feeling as if it was the first time he'd ever made love to a woman.

They held each other, reluctant to separate. Maddy slipped her leg from over his, but they were still joined.

He kissed her lips lightly, feeling her breath as she sighed. "Are you okay?"

"Yes," she whispered. "I've waited a long time," she said, thrilled by the freedom to touch him intimately. His cheek was smooth from shaving a few hours before, and she brushed his wet hair behind his ear. "You look so different without your hat on."

"A cowboy always takes off his hat before he makes love to his woman."

"'His woman'?"

"Yeah. And don't forget it."

He was imbedded within her. How could she forget anything? "I don't think I could," she managed. There was absolutely nothing about this vacation she would forget.

"That was incredible," he said, nuzzling her neck. "It's been a very long time since anything, any*one*, has affected me this way. Thank you, Maddy."

She smiled. "You're welcome."

He began to chuckle, and carefully withdrew from her. Maddy rolled onto her back and closed her eyes against the flash of sunlight that peeked through the tree branches. She was pleasantly sore, yet she wouldn't want to climb on a horse anytime in the near future.

Stuart left the shaded haven, returning a few minutes later with his shirt. He knelt beside her and gently washed the slight traces of blood from her thighs. "Did I hurt you?"

"Not really." He was careful and kind, and her heart wanted to burst with love for him. He didn't look as if he believed her. "Well, only for a minute."

He tossed the shirt aside, and lay down beside her again. He traced the shape of her lips with his finger. "Don't look at me that way, Maddy."

"What way?"

"As if you cared."

"I can't help caring," she protested softly. *Or loving.*

"I can't give you anything in return."

"I couldn't make love to someone I didn't care about."

He hesitated, then kissed her lips. "Neither could I, Maddy." He sighed, as if he hated to admit it. "Neither could I."

"Know what I'd like to do now? Something else I've never done before."

Disappointment clouded his blue eyes. "We just used the only condom," he cautioned.

She smiled. "We don't need one to go skinny-dipping."

"You remember how cold that water is?"

"It wasn't that bad." She sat up and rubbed her cheek on his warm shoulder.

"Because I warmed you up afterward."

She scrambled to her feet and took his hand. "You afraid?"

He looked insulted, which she'd counted on. "Afraid of what?"

"Someone will see us?"

"There's no one around here," he protested.

She tugged him toward the water. "Come on, cowboy. We're going to take a bath in the ol' waterin' hole."

They played together for the rest of the morning. When their clothes were dry, which didn't take long in the heat, they put them on and returned to trying to catch an elusive fish so Jenna and Mac wouldn't doubt they'd spent their hours together fishing.

Maddy lucked out and hooked a fish. A little on the small side, it was still a good fish to take a picture of. A good fish to cook for dinner if you weren't very hungry, Stuart teased. After a while he took her hand and led her back along the stream bank to find Mac and Jenna.

Still surprised by the feelings she aroused in him, Stuart gripped Maddy's hand. He was strangely unwilling to let her go, even when they approached Mac's fishing spot. But Maddy tugged her hand free before either Jenna or Mac noticed anything different.

Jenna looked up from her book. "I caught one," she announced.

Maddy held up the container that held her prize. "So did I!"

Mac reeled in his line. "Fish for dinner tonight," he said with satisfaction. "It was a darn good mornin'."

He looked up at Stuart and grinned. "How'd you do? Catch anything?"

Stuart remembered the way Maddy's body had felt surrounding him. He could close his eyes and feel her skin and inhale the light scent of her perfume. "No," he answered.

"Fish not bitin', eh? Guess you didn't bring any luck with you, boy."

"I wouldn't say that," Stuart replied, glancing toward Maddy. She blushed and turned to Jenna, who held up the book to show her how much she'd read. Fishing was the last thing on his mind. Going back to the ranch, getting work out of the way, and being with Maddy tonight were all he could think about.

IT WAS GOING TO BE easier than he thought, Stuart realized. The phone rang the minute they walked in the door. Jenna was invited to spend the night with Melissa, who lived between the ranch and Lordsburg, off Highway 80. Which also meant, as Stuart pointed out with a particularly satisfied expression, they'd have the house to themselves for the night.

So Maddy changed her clothes, took the big car and drove her there, talked to Melissa's mother, and promised Jenna she'd pick her up Sunday afternoon at four o'clock.

Maddy looked into those silver-blue eyes of his and could hardly wait. She'd memorized the way his body fit into hers, the way his lips teased her skin, the fresh male scent of him when she licked that hollow beneath his earlobe. She'd done the unthinkable—fallen in love with a cowboy—and she didn't know what she was going to do about it except...enjoy it. It certainly would never happen again, not in Connecticut, anyway.

And when school started and it was time to go back to her "real" life, well, at least she'd have something wonderful to remember. She didn't know if this was love or lust—the real thing or a simple summer infatuation.

It didn't matter, she reminded herself. Today, and tonight, he was hers.

"THIS COULD BE HABIT-forming," Maddy said, accepting the frosty glass from Stuart.

"A lot of things could." He sat beside her in the lounge chair facing the pool. Starlight reflected off the still water, and a sliver of moon angled above them.

"I've never had so much to drink in my entire life."

"I don't think one margarita every other night is going to hurt you, Maddy."

"You've taught me to drink beer, too."

"Only to wash the salsa down."

"True. I'll keep telling myself that." She took a sip of the drink and leaned back in the chair. "I love looking at the stars. I don't know why they don't look like this in New England."

They sat in silence and looked at the sky until Stuart reached over and took her hand. "Finish your drink, Maddy."

She took the last swallows and set the glass on the tile. "Finished."

"Good." He stood and pulled her to her feet. "We have some unfinished business from this morning."

"Unfinished?"

"Yes," he said, swinging her into his arms and holding her tightly against him. "There's definitely more to learn."

She kissed his chin. "And you're just the person to teach me?"

"Yeah."

When he'd finished kissing her, she smiled up at him. "Yippee."

He guided her toward the door to the living room. "You took the words right out of my mouth."

This time, in the comfort of Stuart's wide bed, he made love to her with his mouth and lips and tongue until Maddy, amazed by the variety of sensations he aroused, felt the need to reciprocate. She trailed her lips along his chest, and lower, to linger at his abdomen. She took him into her mouth gently, afraid she would hurt him, until his moans of pleasure assured her differently.

He paused, pulled her up on top of him, and she took him inside her. There was no pain this time, just pure pleasure as his hard length stroked her. The slight soreness became sweet sensation as Stuart tumbled her onto her back and made love to her with long, insistent strokes. Her body cried for release, and she gripped his shoulders as she trembled around him.

Soon he followed, riding her to his own climax until he gasped Maddy's name against her throat.

10

"GOOD MORNING," a husky male voice murmured close to her ear. It was followed by a kiss on her bare shoulder, making Maddy shiver. Rough palms slid over her breasts and lower, pulling her against a hard male arousal. Maddy wriggled, still not opening her eyes, intrigued by this new way of waking in the morning. Stuart tugged her onto her back and slid gently over her.

Maddy opened her eyes and looked up at him. "What are you doing?"

He kissed her neck. "You'll find out in a second."

"Are you trying to tell me it's time to get up and fix your breakfast?"

"I don't want breakfast," he said, pushing her thighs apart with a smooth motion. "Not yet, anyway."

"No bacon and eggs?" she teased, wondering if he sensed how easily he sent her senses spinning. Already she wanted him as much as she had last night. She ran her hands along his back as he fit himself easily inside her.

"No." He moved within her, sliding his length until he almost withdrew, then slipping himself into her again with an easy and sensual movement.

"Pancakes?" she breathed, holding on to his waist.

He smiled—a lazy smile that matched the slow, tantalizing motion of his body inside hers. "No."

"French toast?"

"No, sweetheart." He drove deeper, making Maddy gasp against his shoulder. "It's Sunday, your...day off. Remember?"

After last night, Maddy knew she was lucky she could remember she was in New Mexico. She smoothed her hands along his back and pulled him closer. He filled her again and again, making slow, tender love to her until exquisite sensation spiraled between them and overcame them both.

"I have to work this morning," he said much later, as Maddy snuggled against his hard shoulder. "I'll try to be done after lunch sometime. We can go for a swim, or work on your roping technique. Your choice." He kissed the top of her head and eased away from her, tucking the sheet over her bare body. "Go back to sleep."

"I'll get up, too," she murmured, but she didn't move or open her eyes.

"Stay where you are. You have the whole day to do what you want."

She didn't answer, so he got up and watched her sleep. It was strange seeing her in his bed, as if she'd always been there and not across the courtyard. Her dark hair tumbled over the pillows and, despite the air-conditioning, the faint scent of her perfume lingered in the room. One beautiful, smooth, female shoulder peeked from under the covers, and he resisted the urge to put his lips to the bare skin. He knew if he started, he wouldn't stop.

He couldn't spend all day making love to her, no matter how tempting the thought. But he wouldn't mind sitting on the edge of the bed and watching her sleep. If he was a less practical man, that's exactly what he would do. But there were chores to be assigned, a sick horse to doctor and a hundred other necessary jobs to accomplish before sundown.

Stuart found his clothes, then turned back to the woman in his bed. He moved silently toward her, wondering if he could kiss her goodbye without waking her. He contented himself with touching a dark curl outlined on the pillow. That would have to be enough for now. After all, he told himself, moving quickly to the bathroom to dress, he was a very busy man.

At least until this afternoon. The thought cheered him, and he had to make a conscious effort not to whistle.

"WHERE IS SHE?" a woman's shrill voice called. "Why are you hiding her from me?" There was a pause, then the voice grew louder. "I told you, Harry, we should have brought the lawyer. But no, you said it wouldn't be necessary. How *necessary* is it now, Harold?"

Stuart's voice cut in. "Now, Irene—"

"Don't use that tone of voice on me, Stuart Anderson. I want to see my granddaughter. And I want to see her *now. Right now.*"

Maddy stepped out of the kitchen, curious to see the people who were making such a commotion in the living room. She wiped her hands on a checked dishtowel and peered down the hall. So much for an intimate afternoon with Stuart by the pool. The people talking were obviously Jenna's grandparents. The woman's querulous voice hurt her ears.

Stuart answered, his voice low, his expression thunderous. "Jenna's at a friend's house, Irene. I'm picking her up in a couple of hours, so you'll see her then. If I'd known you were coming—"

"You'd have locked the doors," the silver-haired woman finished for him. "And it wouldn't be the first time."

"And this wouldn't be the first time you've barged in here demanding everything under the sun, either. I've never locked you out, but it's not too late to start."

Maddy took two steps backward, hoping to retreat to the kitchen before anyone saw her. The kitchen looked like a pretty good place to hide; if nothing else, it was close to her bedroom, which was an even better hideaway.

"Who's this?" the older man demanded, suspicion in his eyes as he caught a glimpse of Maddy standing in the doorway. "She your newest lady friend?"

Stuart shot Maddy an apologetic look, then turned back to Harold. "Watch it, Harry. I'd like you to meet Madeleine Harmon, the new housekeeper."

"*Housekeeper?*" Irene cackled. "If she's a housekeeper, I'm Princess Diana."

"Maddy, these people are Jenna's grandparents, Irene and Harry Newman."

"Nice to meet you." Maddy thought about extending her hand, but thought better of it. The two older people, suntanned, with shining gray hair and matching aqua-and-white jogging suits, looked as if they didn't shake hands with the hired help. They didn't even look as if they *spoke* to the hired help. Stuart's jaw tightened, and Maddy tried to avoid an explosion. "If you'll excuse me, I have something on the stove that needs to be stirred."

"Nice touch," Irene sniffed.

Stuart glared at the his former mother-in-law. "Don't worry, Irene. You won't be invited to stay for dinner."

"We've made other plans for the evening, if you'll allow Jenna to join us for dinner," her husband replied. "We wouldn't dream of intruding."

Maddy backed into the kitchen. Intruding was obviously what Stuart's in-laws were very good at. She stood out of sight and listened to the conversation.

"What do you mean, Harold? We're not intruding, and we're not going anywhere. The housekeeper can cook dinner. I want to see my granddaughter," Irene declared. "And I'm sure Connie would have wanted us to be treated hospitably. Is our old room still available?"

There was dead silence. Finally Stuart answered. "You can have my room."

"And where will you sleep? Not in the barn, surely."

Stuart ignored the pointed question. "You have two hours to wait for Jenna. I'm picking her up at four."

Maddy heard the door slam and wondered who had walked out, until she heard the voices in the living room. Irene and Harold must be making themselves at home while Stuart stomped off outside.

Well, it looked like she'd better make up Stuart's bed for Harry and Irene. She didn't want to go through the living room and have to run the risk of them speaking to her, so she went out through the kitchen and across the courtyard. The pool water glistened invitingly but Maddy kept walking. Maybe later she and Jenna would have a quick swim after dinner. That is, if the grandparents didn't do something to upset Jenna as much as they'd upset Stuart.

With the way they behaved, Maddy had her doubts. But why the antagonism between the Stuart and his in-laws? Wouldn't it be better to be a family, especially when it seemed that they were all each other had?

She went into Stuart's room through the patio doors and stood there, remembering last night. They'd made love for hours, discovering each other's most intimate secrets. She knew now what places on his body he loved having her touch, and he knew how and where to touch her to make her tremble with surprising passion.

Passion. Who would have thought she would discover passion along with roping and riding?

Well, as long as Stuart's in-laws were here, she'd better concentrate on being a housekeeper. She eyed the rumpled bed and wished she and Stuart were alone again. She'd liked waking up with him, surprised herself by drifting off to sleep after they'd made love and then slept until after ten o'clock.

Thank goodness no one had come into the house while she was sleeping. Something told her that Jenna's grandparents were going to bring nothing but trouble.

"YER GETTIN' THE HANG of it there, Miss Maddy."

Maddy walked toward the fence post and unlooped the rope from it. "Thanks, Mac. I've been practicing every chance I can get."

He leaned on the railing and nodded his approval. "I can tell."

"Really?" She tipped the brim of her hat back and coiled the rope once again as she stepped into the middle of the corral. "I can rope the post almost every other time."

"Yeah, I was watchin'. You're a regular Annie Oakley." He looked back over his shoulder toward the house. "They still here?"

"The Newmans?" Mac nodded. "As far as I know.

Stuart went to get Jenna. They said they weren't leaving until they saw her, and then the next thing I knew they're staying here at the ranch."

"God-awful people," Mac muttered. "Can't leave well enough alone."

"Stuart didn't seem real happy to see them." She swung, threw and missed. "Darn it!" She retrieved the rope and tried again, this time successfully placing the loop.

"Hafta try a calf next time."

"A moving target?" Maddy considered it. "Maybe."

"Lemme give you a piece of advice, gal."

Maddy joined him at the railing. "I'm listening," she urged, ready to improve her roping by following any kind of instructions. She was determined to show Stuart that a gal from the East could learn to rope and ride just as well as anyone born on a ranch. Well, she amended, *almost* as well.

"Stay as far away from those people as you can git," he drawled. "That's what I do. Jest do your best to avoid 'em, especially now."

Maddy frowned. Mac looked so serious. "You mean Jenna's grandparents are that bad?"

"Worse." He grimaced. "No sense at all. And no love lost between them and Stuart. Why he puts up with them, well, I sure don't know. I guess he has his reasons."

"Like what?"

"Not my business to say." The old man shook his head. "Let me know when they're gone. I'm keepin' myself scarce till then." He tipped his hat and walked toward his small cabin. Maddy watched his peculiar bowlegged gait and hoped the old man wouldn't be hiding in his cabin for too long. Maybe after Harry and

Irene saw Jenna, they would be content to go back to wherever they came from.

"ISN'T THIS WONDERFUL?" Jenna danced around the kitchen as Maddy attempted to slice vegetables for the salad. "They came all the way from Los Angeles to see me!"

"Do they visit often?"

"Only a few times since Mom, uh, died." Her face fell. "But they fight with Dad all the time. I don't think they like him very much."

"How could they not like your father?"

Jenna shrugged, her expression troubled, making Maddy wish she had never brought up the subject. "I don't know. They just don't get along."

"What do they fight about?"

"I don't know, but I think it has to do with me."

Maddy wished she could erase the worried expression from Jenna's eyes. "Don't worry, honey. Sometimes adults act like children, too, you know. At least you know that all of them love *you*. That's what they have in common, right?"

Jenna smiled. "Right. And I'm glad we're all together. I wonder how long they're gonna stay?"

"I don't know. You just enjoy it, Jenna."

"Enjoy what?" Stuart asked, coming into the kitchen from the back way. Maddy remembered he'd moved his things into his office. They'd be sharing the bathroom *and* the private wing of the house. She wondered if they'd be sharing a bed tonight, too. She didn't dare look at him too long, for fear she'd start grinning like an idiot.

"Having Harry and Irene here," Jenna explained. "I'm so glad to see them."

Maddy stopped slicing tomatoes. "You call them Harry and Irene?"

"Sure," the child said, waltzing out of the room.

"They told her to," Stuart said, standing closer than she thought necessary. "I think the words *Grandma* and *Grandpa* make them feel old."

"Oh." Maddy couldn't imagine having called her grandfather "Lloyd," but maybe her New England upbringing had been a bit narrow-minded. Stuart touched her back in a private greeting, and Maddy smiled at him. It was hard to keep her mind on the salad when he stood so close to her.

"Smells good in here," he said.

"Beef Burgundy, with white rice, sourdough bread, and a salad. I don't think 'Harry and Irene' will have any complaints."

"I'm sure they won't." He moved away, and lowered his voice. "They're in the living room knocking down another round of gin-and-tonics, so they're feeling no pain."

"How long are they staying?"

"I have no idea. Long enough to torture me, I suppose." He grimaced. "Sorry about this afternoon. I thought it was better if I stayed away from the house, so I drove over to the north section to inspect fences. It was hard to return."

She started to tell him about her roping, but decided to surprise him instead. "That's okay."

"Thanks for making dinner."

"I'm the housekeeper, after all," she said. "Remember?"

"Oh," he replied, stepping closer to kiss her quickly on the lips. "I remember a lot of things."

Maddy blushed. "Dinner's ready. Would you tell your in-laws that it's time to sit down at the table?"

He muttered an oath under his breath. "I should have known I'd have to pay for a day that started off so well." He strode out of the room and returned just as Maddy was spooning the main course into an earthenware bowl. "There are only four places set at the table."

"Mac went into hiding, and I don't think it's appropriate for the housekeeper to join in a family dinner." She set the bowl near the pass-through and retrieved the bread from the oven.

"Appropriate? What the hell kind of talk is that?"

Maddy didn't let his anger bother her. She knew when she was right. "Lower your voice."

"No, damn it." But he dropped his voice. "You're not a servant around here. You never have been."

"I'm the housekeeper," she insisted. "Not your girlfriend. I think it's best that we leave it that way."

He glared at her. "You're the damnedest woman."

"Thank you." She handed him the salad bowl. "You can sweet-talk me later."

"Oh, I'll see you later, all right." He frowned at her again, his glance sweeping her from her sandaled feet to the snug jeans and low, square-necked white T-shirt. "Don't think you're going to get away with this."

"Okay." She picked up the bowl of rice. "Here we go. I'll serve in the dining room and leave you to your happy little family dinner."

He swore and, still holding the salad bowl, turned toward the door. His boots clicked on the tile as he stomped out of the room. "Come and get it!" he yelled.

Maddy followed him into the dining room. She didn't know what was going on, but she was determined to find out. She told herself it was because she needed to help Jenna, but she knew that the secret to Stuart's heart had to be found, too.

"WHY ARE THEY HERE, Stuart?"

Stuart looked up from the pile of paperwork mounded on the makeshift desk to see Maddy silhouetted in the bathroom doorway. "To see Jenna. To torture me." *To take my daughter away.*

She took a step closer. "I hope it's all right that I unlocked this door," she said, motioning toward the bathroom. "Since you're staying here, I mean."

He couldn't believe how beautiful she was. Not a classic cover-model beauty, but a prettiness that surpassed ordinary beauty, he realized. "Come on in," he said. "And of course, I don't mind. I appreciate it, as a matter of fact."

She came in and sat down on a metal chair at the desk. "Working on the books?"

"Sort of."

She peered over to see what the papers were. "I did the payroll records. I started with January and got as far as April."

"You don't have to do that." He sighed. "I'll catch up eventually."

Maddy looked as if she wanted to argue, but changed her mind. "Tell me what's going on, Stuart. Your in-laws are here to make trouble, aren't they?"

"That's nothing new," he answered. He couldn't discuss the custody suit with her. He didn't want her to know that he was on the verge of losing his daughter. He didn't want to see the pity in her eyes. Or the condemnation.

"They've done this before?"

He nodded. "Several times. They arrive, get Jenna all stirred up, talk about Connie for hours, and when they leave Jenna is miserable and I'm back where I started, trying to help her get over her mother's death."

She reached over and took his hand. "I'm sorry."

He gave her hand a squeeze and released it, refusing the offer of sympathy. Refusing the intimacy she offered.

Maddy took the hint. She got up to say good-night, her eyes confused. "See you in the morning."

"Good night," he replied, willing himself to say nothing more than that. She closed the bathroom door behind her, leaving him to his quiet room. He eyed the pile of paperwork in front of him. It really wasn't fair to expect Maddy to keep up with it. She was earning her salary with the cooking and tutoring. The fact that he'd been making love to her complicated the entire situation.

Hell, he should have kept his hands off her. Stuart ran his hand through his hair, knowing that keeping away from Maddy was impossible. He hadn't quite figured out why she appealed to him, but he didn't care to analyze it. He liked the way she talked, appreciated the way her bottom bounced on the saddle, and liked how she'd made the old ranch house seem like a home again.

He'd convinced her to stay until school started, and he couldn't think about what would happen after that.

Stuart pushed the papers aside and stared out the doors at the empty courtyard. He'd call his lawyer first thing in the morning. Having the Newmans in his home could be potentially dangerous to the custody suit. Or would it help by showing the judge that Jenna's grandparents were welcome to visit their granddaughter? He wasn't the kind of monster who would keep them apart, as much as he'd like to. What were Harry and Irene up to, anyway? Snooping around to see if they could find something to destroy him with?

Hiring a housekeeper was supposed to have been the answer to his problems, the answer to his prayers. A womanly influence, a tutor, a companion.

Well, that part had worked. Jenna was happier, and had been doing her schoolwork to the point where it looked as if she'd have no trouble being admitted to sixth grade at the end of the summer. And while Jenna still wasn't as close to him as she used to be, she wasn't snapping at him or even trying to avoid him.

There'd even been glimpses of the affectionate little girl he'd remembered—the one who'd loved him, before her mother died. He didn't know where things had gone wrong after Connie's accident, but Jenna had taken her anger and grief and thrown it at him, as if she blamed him for the accident.

It was hard enough just getting through the days without blaming himself—for not making Connie happy, for not working harder to make the marriage work.

Well, he'd realized it took two people to make a marriage, and Connie hadn't been one of the two. Jenna had talked more to him than his wife, those last couple of years. Until her mother died.

He couldn't help the secret, tiny thread of relief that sneaked up on him at times. He couldn't help the guilt, either. Two things he had to live with. And yet, having Maddy made him forget.

Forget that women couldn't be trusted, forget the

pain of loving someone too much, forget that once he'd been young and full of illusions.

"WELL, YOU CERTAINLY make his life easier around here, don't you?"

Maddy didn't turn around. She'd heard Irene enter the kitchen and braced herself for something unpleasant. She'd never met anyone who had inspired such a reaction. "That's my job," she replied.

"Ah, yes, your *job*."

"There's fresh coffee in the carafe on the dining-room table, and another batch of muffins will be ready in a few minutes." *In other words, Irene, you don't belong in my kitchen.*

"However did he find you?"

That was none of Irene's business. Maddy opened the oven to check the muffins, hoping they'd be done so she would have something to do besides stare at the timer on the stove and wish Stuart's mother-in-law to the devil. Two long days of the Newmans had started to seem like two weeks. Or two years.

"I believe I asked you a question," Irene snapped.

Maddy turned to face her, resigning herself to a conversation she'd tried to avoid. "Excuse me," she said, "I'm busy planning breakfast. How do you like your eggs?"

"I don't. Too much cholesterol."

Maddy opened the refrigerator and took out a bowl of fruit salad. "I'll put this on the table and you can help yourself."

"Lovely."

She still stood there when Maddy returned to the kitchen. Like a hawk eyeing a juicy little field mouse,

Irene tried again. "You were telling me how you happened to be working here?"

"I've always wanted to live on a ranch," she began, cracking eggs into a bowl as she spoke. "So I was happy for the opportunity to find work in a place like this."

"Very clever of him," Irene muttered. "Especially now. I suppose you think he's a *decent* man, don't you?" Irene's lips curved into a sarcastic smile.

"Irene, I don't—"

Irene interrupted. "And you've *years* of experience as a housekeeper, I suppose?"

"Several years, as a matter of fact."

"She's also the bookkeeper," Stuart added, stepping into the kitchen. "Is there anything else you'd like to know about my employees, Irene?"

She shook her head, but her blue eyes examined Stuart's angry expression. "I've heard enough about your...employees." She made the last word sound suspect.

"Good." He poured himself a cup of coffee from the pot next to the stove. "Then maybe you'll leave Maddy alone to do her job."

"Breakfast is set up in the dining room," Maddy reminded her. The timer buzzed, and she turned the knob to Off. Irene moved toward the door. "I'll find Jenna so she can join me for breakfast."

"She was out in the barn a while ago."

"Oh." Irene looked pained. "You let her run around like some sort of cowboy. Do you ever know where she is?"

"I told you," he said through gritted teeth. "She's out in the barn. She has chores in the morning, then she and Maddy usually ride before it gets too hot."

"Ah, yes," the woman went on. "More cowboy activities. She's growing up, Stuart. She needs more than horses and saddles and running wild around this ranch."

"Like makeup lessons and beauty pageants, I suppose."

"Connie had no complaints about the way she was brought up." Irene moved toward the door, but before she left she spun around for one last remark. "She would *hate* the way her daughter is turning out, running around like a wild Indian with no discipline and no supervision."

"Jenna is doing just fine."

"She couldn't even pass fifth grade."

"She's making up her work."

"We'll see," Irene sniffed. "I don't believe it for a minute."

"Go have your breakfast, Irene," Stuart said wearily. "We've said this all before."

"It bears repeating," Irene muttered, leaving the doorway.

Stuart clamped his lips together in an effort to keep from saying something he'd regret. His lawyer had warned him that the Newmans would provoke fights. He'd also told him to try and keep the peace, hoping that a settlement could be reached without having to go to court.

Stuart knew there was no chance for compromise. He wouldn't back down an inch. He turned to Maddy, who stirred the scrambled eggs at the stove. "Sorry you had to hear all that."

She shook her head. "Don't worry about me. It's Jenna who doesn't need to hear that kind of talk. She's doing so well right now."

"I don't know how much more of this I can take." He leaned against the counter, his coffee cup forgotten beside him. "I promised you a camping trip, didn't I?"

"Yes, but I'm not in any—"

"Thursday afternoon we'll drive north of Silver City to the Gila National Forest. There's lot of places there to camp. We'll take Jenna and Mac, and Jenna can bring a friend."

"What about Harry and Irene?"

"They're not invited." He almost smiled. "If they won't leave us, then we'll leave them."

"Brilliant idea, cowboy."

"Then you'll go?"

She nodded. "If you'll loan me a sleeping bag."

"You can use mine."

"Okay." She grinned at him.

"Yippee," he said, wishing he could lean over and kiss her. He hadn't touched her since their unexpected company arrived. The last thing he needed was for Irene to portray the ranch as some sort of cowboy-housekeeper orgy.

JENNA WAVED AS THE BIG Cadillac drove down the ranch road, little spurts of dust in its wake. Stuart stood beside the child, an unreadable expression on his face.

Maddy watched from the porch, no closer to knowing the problems between the families than she'd been five days before when the Newmans arrived on the doorstep.

Stuart refused to talk about it, and his face never gave away his feelings. The man must be a killer poker player, for no one could know what he was thinking. He touched the child's shoulder in what looked like a gesture of comfort, but she pulled away from him and ran across the yard into the largest barn.

11

"WELL, WHAT DO YOU think?"

It was the kind of panorama she'd seen in old John Wayne movies. Distant jagged mountains of brown and red, scantily forested hills, and below, the golden desert floor spread beneath them. It was exactly like in the books, too, with the wide blue sky overhead and the feeling that nothing had changed in hundreds of years.

"It's beautiful," was all she could manage to say to Stuart, who stood on the plateau beside her.

He pointed out the different mountain ranges, naming them one by one, but Maddy couldn't absorb it all. Again, like the heroine in Louis Grey's *The Lights of the Desert Stars*, she stood in a similar glade of pines as if she were on top of the world, her protective cowboy beside her.

It was enough to make a woman want to cry. Instead, she took at least ten pictures of this particular New Mexico sunset. Maybe she'd have one enlarged to poster size.

"There are some sunsets that make you think you've landed in heaven," she murmured.

"What?"

"You said that to me once. That first day, driving out to the ranch."

"Well, I was right, wasn't I?"

"Yes. You were right." She'd thought that was pretty poetic for a cowboy. Now, as she stood here, she realized how true his words had been. If this wasn't heaven, she didn't know what was. Unless she counted making love to Stuart Anderson, and waking in his arms.

"The girls are tired," he pointed out, watching as they sat roasting marshmallows by the camp fire. Margaret Jackson had allowed Peggy to join them on the camping trip, which had pleased everyone. Jenna and the tiny redhead found a lot to giggle about, although Stuart and Maddy had no idea what set them off into gales of laughter.

"They've had a busy day."

"But a fun one."

"I thought you were going to buy out Silver City this afternoon."

"I needed a few souvenirs," she protested. They'd stopped at Silver City and done some sight-seeing. Maddy bought lots of postcards, several history books, and Silver City T-shirts for the girls. Billy the Kid had once roamed the area, and Maddy hounded Stuart until he stopped at Billy's boyhood home and his mother's grave.

She was glad she'd brought along four rolls of film. Maybe if she took enough pictures she would convince herself she was still on vacation, still only a temporary visitor in the West, and that she would leave by September with no regrets, without looking back, happy with her freedom and her lack of responsibilities.

And maybe the sun would set in the east tomorrow, too.

His arm came around her shoulder. "What are you thinking?"

She moved away slightly, although she didn't want to. "The girls will see."

"They're busy," he countered.

Maddy looked over. Sure enough, the girls were intent upon their marshmallows and their chatter. "I was thinking about the sunset and how different it is from New England." *I was thinking how much I love making love to you.*

"I'm going to put the tents up. Yours is the big one. You'll be over in that little glade over there. The girls are going to take the small one."

"What about you? Are you alone sleeping under the stars?" She hid her disappointment. Of course cowboys preferred fresh air and bedrolls. He'd probably use his saddle for a pillow, although she couldn't imagine that being comfortable.

"No," Stuart declared, his hand caressing Maddy's shoulder. "I've decided I hate sleeping alone."

"Since when?"

"Since Harry and Irene arrived and ruined my plans to keep you in my bed."

"That wouldn't have worked anyway," she said. "Not with Jenna in the house."

"I know," he agreed. "But we would have found a way somehow."

"You mean like going camping?"

"Or fishing."

She couldn't help flushing at the reminder. "I liked fishing."

"So did I."

"It was very...educational."

He looked as if he wanted to kiss her, but a burst of laughter from the camp fire altered his expression. "I think I'd better go put up the tents."

"Need help?"

He shook his head. "The girls can help. In fact, they can erect their own."

"Maybe that's something else I should learn," she suggested, smiling up at him.

"Come on, then." He started to take her hand, but Maddy wouldn't let him. "I don't want Jenna to get the wrong idea," she said. "Especially when she's been doing so well."

"Because of you," he said, walking beside her back to the fire. "Not even her grandparents could upset her for long."

"Did they try?"

"They want her to move to California and live with them, so they tell her it's what her mother would have wanted."

Maddy shook her head. "No wonder the child's angry. She doesn't know where she belongs."

"She belongs with me," Stuart growled. "And she always will."

MADDY WASN'T SURE she liked camping. The musty smell of canvas surrounded her, and the night noises were strange and unnerving to a naked woman in a nylon sleeping bag. She shivered in the cool night air and burrowed deeper in her sleeping bag, hoping Stuart could join her. If he didn't come soon she'd have to pull on a sweatshirt and leggings. If she slept alone she'd most likely have nightmares.

He came to her long after dark, when all of the ghost stories had been told, the girls were silent in their tent and the traces of the fire had been kicked over by the dusty boot of a man who waited to join his woman.

"It's only me," he said, easing the tent flap open and bending over through the small opening.

"Thank goodness," she whispered. "I don't think I'd make a very good cowboy."

"Why not?" Stuart unbuttoned his shirt and slipped off the rest of his clothes. The darkness was thick around them as Maddy lifted the edge of the sleeping bag so Stuart could slide in beside her.

"I'd get lonesome riding the range all by myself, and I'm not sure I like being alone in a tent." He smelled like sunlight and pine trees, and his skin was warm. The nights without him had been long and lonely. It was amazing how she'd been spoiled by their one night together.

"You're shivering," he said, running his large hand over her shoulder and down her arm. "Come here." He slipped his arm underneath her so she could use his shoulder as a pillow and snuggle against him.

She didn't stop to wonder why she felt so comfortable with him, or question the rush of sensual awareness that shook her whenever he was close to her, or his skin brushed against hers or his eyes met her gaze with that silvery, sexy expression. She didn't want to think about what lay in store after September or even the day after tomorrow. She simply wanted to feel him against her and inside her and around her.

Maddy moved over his hard body. She wanted to smell him on her skin and taste him on her lips and feel him in her mouth.

And a long time later, when they'd finished making long, silent love to each other in the darkness of the starry New Mexico night, Stuart pulled her on top of him, cradling her against him.

She tucked her head under his chin and slept until

dawn. He shifted, waking her without meaning to. He kissed her gently, and tucked her into the sleeping bag. "Go back to sleep," he whispered.

"Love you," she murmured, her eyes closing as she turned on her side away from him.

He paused and stared down at her. There was something so intriguingly vulnerable about a sleeping woman. Especially one who talks in her sleep.

Love you? She couldn't possibly love him, or even think she loved him. It wouldn't work, would only complicate a simple summer.

Hell, he swore to himself as he climbed into his clothes. There was nothing simple about this. *Love you.* Two words that didn't have to mean anything. Except, he realized as he looked back at the sleeping woman, he'd fallen in love with Madeleine Harmon. Which was why he bent over backward to please her, and missed her in his bed when she wasn't there, and made up reasons to walk into the kitchen to see her smile, and why sitting with her by the pool made his nights glow with contentment.

And why making love with her was different from anything he'd ever known.

He slipped out of the tent and into the pale gray morning. It was a good time to build a fire and make a pot of coffee and ignore the fact that he'd fallen seriously in love.

It wasn't like he had to do anything about it, he assured himself. She would be staying on the ranch for a few more weeks. He didn't have to marry her, or anything drastic like that. He didn't have to do a damn thing but try not to make a fool of himself.

He didn't know if that would be easy or hard.

SHE COULDN'T BELIEVE she'd said it. *Love you* had just slipped out, and she didn't have to open her eyes to guess his reaction. She'd heard his breathing stop, sensed his withdrawal. So she'd turned away and pretended to be asleep while he dressed and left the tent. Maybe he'd think it was a dream she was having, something that had nothing to do with him.

The night had been dreamlike, after all. Their bodies continued to fit together with a hunger that overwhelmed her. Maybe a man like Stuart was accustomed to that kind of passion, but Maddy didn't think so. She'd seen the surprise and appreciation in his eyes when he looked down at her, when their bodies were still joined together.

Words couldn't be spoken. She'd be leaving in a few short weeks. Until then, she'd keep her mouth shut and her heart insulated. Stuart Anderson and his daughter needed her, but that didn't mean she had to fall in love with them. And even if she had, it didn't mean she had to change her plans and stay here on the Triple J.

Loving Stuart didn't have to change her life.

"SHORE INTERESTIN' THE way things are goin' around here."

Stuart ignored the old man and kept his head under the hood of the truck.

"First you went on a sunrise ride, then next thing I see you teachin' her how to rope. Then you spend an awful long time fishin' and not catchin' nothin' but great big smiles, then you all go campin'." He shook his head in mock confusion. "What's next, Stuart?"

"Don't know," he answered, wiping his hands on a dirty rag. "New spark plugs and an oil change, I guess."

Mac chuckled. "You're changing a lot of things around here, and it ain't just the oil."

"Stop your gabbing, old man. I've got too much on my mind to listen to you all day long."

"Two weeks ago you were doing some pretty cozy camping with Miss Maddy. And you've been comin' to dinner on time ever since."

"So?" Stuart made a point of putting his head closer to the engine. Maybe if he looked occupied, Mac would quit his jawing and leave him alone.

It didn't work. Mac edged closer, his blue eyes sparkling with mischief. "Anything you want to tell me?"

"No."

"How long is she stayin'?"

"Until school starts."

"Then you're gonna let that little gal leave?"

Stuart turned to Mac and frowned. "I don't have much to say about it."

"What the hell does that mean? You just ask her to stay, that's all."

Stuart shook his head. "She has other plans."

"Like what?"

"The Ripple K Guest Ranch."

The old man swore. "I thought she forgot all about that dude-ranch business."

"I don't think so."

"Have you *asked* her to stay?"

Stuart didn't answer. Of course, he hadn't. He knew what her answer would be. Same thing she'd said a month ago.

"Well, if that don't beat all!" He shook his head as if he didn't know what to do with the younger man. "Hell, if you ain't the dumbest cowboy I ever laid eyes on!"

"Yeah? Why's that?"

"Women like to be asked, boy. They like to be sweet-talked."

"Well, I've never been good at talking."

"You must be good at something." Mac chuckled. "She shore smiles at you a lot."

"Here's the trouble," he declared, hoping to distract the old man. He tapped the spark plug with the wrench. "I'll bet that's the problem right there."

Mac shook his head. "Your problem is you don't know a good thing when you've got it."

Stuart couldn't argue with him. After what Connie had put him through, it was hard to trust his own judgment again. Hard to trust, period. "And sometimes people want to take away what you've already got."

Mac grew quiet. Then he asked, "When's the hearing?"

"Friday."

"Does Jenna know?"

"Not yet." Stuart ignored the look of sympathy Mac gave him.

"She ain't gonna take it real well."

"No, I don't think she is. And if the judge asks her where she wants to live, I don't know what she'll say."

"This ranch is her home, boy. The only one she's ever known."

Stuart shrugged. "And she hasn't been happy."

"Sure, she has. Girls are just funny that way. It's hard to tell if they're happy or not."

"I hope you're right." He went back to the motor. "Don't you have any work to do?"

"Naw," he replied. "Straightenin' you out is a full-time job."

"You should never have retired. You've got too much time on your hands."

"Guess I don't want to go back to housekeepin'," he drawled. "Miss Maddy does one heck of a job with peach pie."

"*You* marry her, then," Stuart said, giving the spark plug a strong twist.

Mac looked startled, then he grinned. "Who's talkin' about gettin' married, boy? I'm just tellin' you to get her to stay on at the Triple J."

"I told you, she won't stay."

"Then marry her." He nodded, pleased with the suggestion. "After all, she's about as far away from Connie as you'll ever get."

"I'M GOING TO MISS YOU, Maddy." Jenna paddled her air mattress closer to Maddy's as they floated in the pool. Homer lay in the shade of the patio table and stared at them. "I wish you wouldn't go."

"I'll miss you, too," Maddy answered. "You've done a good job these past weeks. Aren't you proud of yourself?"

Jenna grinned. "You should have seen Mrs. Butler's face when she saw my book reports!"

"She's the principal?"

"Yeah. She couldn't believe it."

"Neither can I," Maddy said. "You really worked hard, once you put your mind to it."

"All my friends would be in sixth and I'd still be in fifth. I'd hate that."

"I'll bet." Maddy tried not to laugh. Jenna and her new girlfriends were on the phone together so much, she'd had to put a time limit on the phone calls. She wondered why Stuart hadn't complained yet. He was most likely happy that Jenna was so cheerful and had also been promoted to sixth grade. "Your father told me he had a very good meeting at the school."

"I wish you didn't have to leave when school starts. Do you have to?"

"Yes, honey, I have to. I think I've been here long enough." *Long enough to fall in love with your father and turn my world upside down.*

"But school starts in seven days," she moaned. "I still need you."

Maddy shook her head. "Not with your schoolwork, you don't. You'll do fine. You're a smart girl, and you can get good grades when you work hard and don't fight with your father."

"I was really mean to him," she confessed.

"Now you know he didn't deserve that, don't you?"

"Yeah, I know." Jenna grinned. "But he's a lot nicer now that you're here."

"Jenna—"

"It's true!" The child laughed.

Maddy wished she could roll right off the mattress and into the water. If Jenna continued talking like this, she'd have to do just that. "I'm sure your father was nice all the time. You just didn't notice."

Jenna's expression grew wistful. "I wish you could stay here forever, Maddy."

Time to hit the water, Maddy decided, so Jenna wouldn't notice the tears that had sprung so suddenly to her eyes. She slipped into the water with a small splash and heard Jenna squeal as the cool water hit her.

Maddy surfaced and pushed the hair out of her face. Seven days left to pretend she wasn't in love with Jenna's father. Seven days to disguise her feelings and swallow the words she longed to say.

It wasn't going to be easy. She and Stuart had fallen into a comfortable pattern these past weeks. They drank margaritas or iced tea by the pool at night, and made love whenever they could get the time alone. Stuart had moved back into his bedroom once the Newmans left, but the fact that he worked in his office next to her bedroom made it easier for them to have time together.

And that time together was almost over. She didn't know where the days had gone, but it was over too quickly.

She waved to Jenna, who paddled closer. "How many days did you say it was until school starts?"

"Seven."

"Guess we'd better go shopping for school clothes."

Jenna made a face. "Why did I have to remind you?"

"Sorry, kid." Maddy splashed water at her. "You're stuck with me for a little while longer." Jenna splashed back and Maddy retaliated with a bigger splash until Jenna tumbled off the mattress and joined Maddy in the water while Homer barked from the safety of the table.

"Dad!" Jenna called, and Maddy looked over as Stuart stepped into the courtyard. He wore his work clothes and looked hot and tired.

One week, she thought, after Jenna climbed out of the pool to greet her father. Seven days to look at that magnificent man and not tell him she loved him.

Seven days to pretend it wouldn't be hell to leave him.

She knew she couldn't possibly stay. She had to get on with her life, and staying on as a housekeeper for the Andersons would merely postpone the fact that Madeleine Harmon had to find a life of her own.

Up until now she'd been treading water. Maybe she should leave now while she still could. She waved to Stuart. Tonight she'd tell him she should leave this weekend.

Stuart stood by the pool and wished he'd taken time to clean up before seeing the women. Once Mac had stopped talking, he'd been able to finish up with the motor in no time. Marry Maddy? What in hell could Mac have been thinking? *Marry* her?

Marriage was too drastic a solution for keeping a housekeeper around.

He certainly didn't need to do anything so permanent, just because he needed her around. Except for the fact that he loved her. Or thought he loved her. How in hell did a man know for sure? He'd thought he was in love with his first wife, and look where that had gotten him: right into a passel of trouble that was still going on.

Except, when he thought about Maddy leaving the Triple J, such black despair filled him that he couldn't breathe.

Unaware of his thoughts, Maddy waved to him, her face turning up to him in a pleased smile. Similar to the expression she wore when they made love. His stomach tightened as he waved back. Damn it all, what was he going to do?

"School starts next week," was the only thing he could think to say.

"I know," she answered, paddling close to him. "Jenna and I were just talking about it. I'm going to take her into town tomorrow for school clothes."

"I'll leave some money out for you. Make sure she gets a decent dress and shoes to match." She'd need

something for court, something feminine and new.
Something to impress the judge.

"Okay. Any special occasion?"

"Not really." *Only to look good in front of the judge who
would decide the course of her life.* "Just make sure she
gets it." He ignored Maddy's surprised expression. He
couldn't tell her the truth, although he didn't know
how he could avoid it much longer. He couldn't stand
her pity, and he didn't want her to worry. This was his
problem, and his alone.

The knot in his stomach expanded and tightened. He
could lose Jenna the day after tomorrow, and lose
Maddy next week. He couldn't imagine what his life
would be like with both of them gone.

Or was Mac right? Was Maddy waiting to be asked
to stay?

STUART TRIED TO SAY the words when he and Maddy
were saddling the horses after dinner, but Jenna interrupted with a question and invited herself along on
their sunset ride.

He attempted to ask the question in the privacy of
the barn, when he thought they were alone. Then one
of the hands rounded the corner, spouting off about a
sick calf. The moment had been effectively destroyed.

Still determined, he resolved to find a better spot.
Margaritas by the pool under the romantic haze of the
desert stars seemed like a winner. Until Homer's fren-
zied barking broke the mood.

And in the private quiet of her bedroom, words and
questions were no longer necessary. Hours later, Stuart
knew this could be his chance. If he didn't blow it, that
is. If no cowhands, kids or dogs ran through the room.
After all, he wasn't some lily-livered coward going

through life cowering in the mesquite. If Maddy stayed, she'd become Mrs. Anderson and everything would go on as before. Only better, because he wouldn't ever have to worry about her leaving him.

"Maddy?" She lay in the crook of his arm, a warm naked woman tucked neatly against his side.

"Hmm..."

"I've been thinking." Stuart grimaced. *Brilliant opening, Anderson.*

She snuggled closer. "Okay," she said in a sleepy voice.

"Maddy, look at me."

She lifted her head. "You sound so serious."

"Well, I—" Then he closed his mouth. How on earth was he going to say this?

"I wanted to talk to you, too," she said, struggling to sit up despite the tangle of sheets that surrounded her. She faced him as he lay on his back with his arms tucked behind his head. "It's about next week. I don't think you need me anymore, especially now that Jenna is caught up for school."

"What are you talking about?"

"Leaving," she answered gently. "It's time."

"No. We agreed that you would work here until school started," he reminded her.

"I know, but—"

"I don't want you to leave."

"I have to." She didn't look happy about the decision, Stuart noted. "It's time, Stuart. It's the end of the summer."

"It doesn't have to be," he growled. "You don't have to go."

"But I do."

"Marry me, Maddy." Once the words were out, he was amazed at how easy it had been to say them.

She stared at him. "What?"

So he said it again. "Marry me, Maddy."

"You don't want to get married."

"How do you know what I want? I'm asking you, to-night, to say you'll marry me."

Motionless, she sat and stared at him. "I don't un-derstand."

"I'll give you a good life here, Maddy. You can have all the sunrise rides and sunsets on the porch and I'll even throw in Snake as a wedding present."

Maddy opened her mouth but no sound came out.

"Speechless," he announced, with some satisfaction. "Must be the first time in your entire life, Madeleine Harmon."

She nodded. "I don't know what to say, or what to think."

He leaned forward and took her small hands in his. "Say yes. Say you'll stay here with us."

She looked down at their clasped hands and then back into Stuart's eyes. "We haven't known each other very long."

"Long enough."

She turned those big brown eyes on him. "I just don't know what to say."

"At least you didn't say no. Sleep on it," he whis-pered, tugging her down against his chest. He wanted to go to sleep knowing she lay beside him.

How could she expect her to sleep after he'd asked her to marry him? Maddy snuggled against his chest, inhaling the warm male scent of him. Marry him? She hadn't dreamed of actually staying here; hadn't dared consider ever being able to stay with the man she'd fallen in love with. He hadn't said he loved her, but she had known all this time that he wasn't a demonstrative man. He wasn't the kind of man whose words came easily.

He loved her. Of that she was certain. There was a certain way he looked at her, a possessive expression in his blue eyes when he touched her.

Marrying Stuart meant living here in New Mexico, on the Triple J, forever. The Madeleine in the Louis Grey book had stayed with her cowboy, too. Did dreams come true in real life, too? Did she dare risk believing in happy endings?

STUART WAS GONE when she woke up the next morning. A glance at the alarm clock told her she'd overslept by two hours. Mac and Stuart had to have made their own coffee and were most likely doing chores by now.

Maddy rolled over and hopped out of bed. She'd take a quick shower and round up Jenna for the trip to town. She peeked into the kitchen first, unwilling to be caught in her robe by any of the cowboys. The room was quiet, a half pot of coffee left on the counter. Maddy poured herself a cup and noticed that whoever had made breakfast had cleaned up after himself. Jenna's cereal bowl was in the sink.

Stuart's chair was pulled out, as if he'd left in a hurry and had forgotten to push it in. She loved those pressed-back chairs, loved the way Stuart hooked his hat on the knob when he sat down to eat.

She wanted to see his hat hooked over the back of the kitchen chair until the day she died. Maddy hurried back to her room to get dressed. She'd take Jenna to town, and then later, when she and Stuart were alone, she'd tell him she'd stay.

12

"WELL? DO YOU LIKE IT?"

Stuart cleared his throat before he answered. "Yes, but do you have to look so grown-up?"

"Oh, Dad!" Jenna shoved the clothes back into the bags. "Wait until Melissa hears about what I got! See ya later." She hurried out of the room, a vision in a blue flowered dress.

Stuart turned to Maddy. "She seems happy."

Maddy grinned. "She had a good time."

"I could tell." He stepped closer and put his hands on her shoulders, looking down into her eyes. "What about you?" He kissed her lightly on the lips. "Did you have a good time, too?"

"Yes." She sighed. "But I'm glad to be home."

"Home?" he repeated, a hopeful expression lighting his face. "Does that mean you're going to stay?"

"Maddy!"

He turned as Jenna bounced back into the kitchen. Maddy stepped out of the circle of his arms as Jenna grinned at her. "What do you want now, kid?"

"I can't get out of this dumb dress." She turned around so Maddy could unhook the top catch.

"There," Maddy said. "You're all set. Make sure you hang it up."

"I will." She turned to her father. "Why do I need this, anyway?"

"I'll tell you later."

"You're sure acting weird."

"I'm a father," Stuart replied, wondering how much longer that would be true. No, he couldn't think that way. He had to believe it would all work out the way it should. "I'm allowed."

Jenna ignored him and left the kitchen. Ignoring the pain in his gut, Stuart pulled Maddy into his arms once again. "Where were we?"

"I don't know where you were, but I'm going to make dinner, then finish up those payroll records."

"When are we getting married?"

"Hold on. I haven't said yes yet."

"Then say it, damn it, and let's make some plans."

She almost laughed. He looked so fierce. "All right, cowboy. *Yes*, it is. Make all the plans you want."

He hesitated, as if he wasn't sure he'd heard correctly. "Yes?"

"Unless you've changed your mind."

Stuart shook his head. "Never, sweetheart. You're mine for a long, long time." He took her into his arms and kissed her as if he would never let her go.

She entered her last number into the appropriate column and hit the Enter key. The computer program tallied the numbers in a matter of seconds and Maddy leaned back in her chair, satisfied that the records had reconciled properly. She turned on the printer and adjusted the paper. Stuart would be surprised when he found out that this job was finally finished.

It hadn't been easy to keep her mind on her work, but she'd been grateful for something to keep her busy. Stuart had been needed by a couple of the cowhands and hadn't returned to the house for dinner, leaving them no time to talk about the wedding plans.

She didn't want a long engagement, and she doubted if he did, either. And she'd prefer a simple ceremony; there was no one except a handful of friends to notify. She didn't know about Stuart, but she guessed something small and private would appeal to him. They had to tell Mac and Jenna, but since he'd been called to the north forty on some kind of emergency, she'd kept her secret and sent Jenna to bed half an hour ago.

When the phone rang she waited, hoping Stuart was in the house to answer it. It rang twice more, so Maddy picked it up. If it was one of Jenna's friends, she'd be told it was too late for phone calls.

"Hello?"

"Let me speak to Stuart."

That demanding tone could only belong to Irene Newman. Maddy curbed her annoyance. "I'm sorry, but he's not available right now."

"Who is this, the housekeeper?"

"This is Madeleine Harmon, yes."

"I was going to give him one last chance to give up. Tell him it's not going to work," she snapped. "He won't fool the judge tomorrow with this housekeeper business. I'll make sure of it."

Maddy had had it with the woman's rudeness. She fought the desire to put her in her place and lost. "I am now Stuart's fiancée, Mrs. Newman."

There was a long, stunned silence. "Damn it, he did it! I knew it'd be just my rotten luck he'd marry you just to spite me." Her voice grew higher. "Tell him his tricks aren't going to work."

"Mrs. Newman, I don't know what—"

"Don't play dumb with me, lady. You know damn well about the custody hearing. Why else would you be getting married except to spite me? Well, it won't work. Jenna belongs with us. Tell that *fiancé* of yours that I'll see him in court tomorrow, and I won't stop until I win, no matter who he bribes to marry him."

Maddy winced as the receiver slammed in her ear. Irene Newman sounded on the verge of a mental collapse. What on earth was the woman talking about? How could there be a custody hearing without Stuart telling her about it? And if it was true, wouldn't Jenna have to know what was going on?

She replaced the receiver and stood, ignoring the blinking light on the monitor. Across the courtyard Stuart's bedroom light glowed, meaning he'd returned to the house. She slipped out of the room and crossed the yard to the veranda and knocked on the wide glass door to Stuart's bedroom.

The room was empty, but she heard his low voice and the surprising sound of Jenna crying. Maddy stepped through his room to the hall and stood in the open doorway of Jenna's room. Stuart sat on the edge of the bed, the child in his arms. Her paperback book lay forgotten on the sheet, and as Maddy watched, Jenna pulled away from her father and huddled by herself with her pillow clutched to her chest.

"What's going on around here?" Maddy asked, wondering at the pain in the child's eyes.

Stuart turned to her, but didn't answer.

"I have to go to court," Jenna wailed. "Harry and Irene want me to live with them."

"It's not going to be so bad," Stuart said, trying to reassure her. "The judge will ask you some questions and —"

"And the *judge* will decide where I hafta live?"

He nodded. "I think that's the way it's going to work." He reached out and brushed a large hand along her hair, smoothing it. "You know I've always wanted to adopt you, but your mother died before the papers were final. Your grandparents want to adopt you, too, so they're going to be in the courtroom tomorrow to tell the judge."

"I'm scared, Maddy. I don't want to go to court."

Maddy stepped into the room and sat on the edge of the bed. Jenna threw herself into Maddy's arms, and Maddy rubbed her back and made soothing noises until the child's sobs stopped.

"Now, listen to me," Maddy ordered, as Jenna sat up and wiped her face. "You're old enough to tell *anyone* what you want to do with your life, even an old judge." Stuart handed her a clean handkerchief and Jenna blew her nose. Maddy continued, "So tomorrow you're going to wear your new dress and march into court beside your father and show the world that you know where you belong."

"That's the trouble, Maddy." She looked up at her with sad eyes. "How do I know where I belong?"

Maddy's heart ached. Leave it to a child to get to the crux of the problem. "Your heart will tell you, honey. All you have to do is listen to it."

She stayed with Jenna until she fell asleep. Stuart walked to the window and stared out at the desert until Maddy slipped off the bed and moved toward the door.

"Maddy," he whispered.

She shook her head, unwilling to talk to him. She'd had time to do some listening herself, and what she'd realized wasn't a pretty sight. From the time she'd arrived at the ranch, Stuart had made it clear he needed a housekeeper.

And he'd got one.

He'd kept one, too, through a combination of sight-seeing, Western charm and male sensuality. Nothing had been spared to keep Madeleine Harmon on the Triple J.

Now she knew why.

"I need a drink," he said, going to the bar in the living room.

"Make two." Alcohol wasn't going to make any difference in her anger or disappointment, but she figured she could always throw the empty glass at him.

He finished dumping the ingredients into the blender and turned it on for a few seconds. He poured half of it into a large glass and handed it to her before filling a shot glass with whiskey.

She sipped at hers; he drank his in one swallow. Then she waited, unsmiling, wondering what he would say, how he would explain.

"Thanks, Maddy" were the last words she expected to hear.

"Thanks?"

"I didn't know how to calm her down."

"You obviously threw a bomb at her. What did you expect, a hug and a kiss good-night?"

He looked stunned. "I thought it would be better if I told her at the last minute, so she wouldn't worry about it. I didn't want to upset her."

"You didn't think she'd need time to understand what was going on? Didn't you think she'd want to talk about it, think about it?"

"No. I was just trying to save her from worrying."

"Perhaps that's what fathers do—protect their little

girls from heartache," she answered slowly. "But why didn't you tell *me* what was going on? I just took a phone call from your mother-in-law."

He swore and poured himself another shot. "*Ex*-mother-in-law."

"You're not going to make a good impression in the courtroom if your eyes are bloodshot."

He slammed the empty glass on the bar and frowned at her. "What's eatin' you, Maddy? I know what *my* problems are, because I might lose my daughter tomorrow, so—"

"You won't lose if you have a fiancée, will you? A nice woman who's a good influence on Jenna, someone to keep house and cook hot meals and drive Jenna to her girlfriend's and help her with her homework. It sure would appear to be one happy little family. It worked out perfectly for you, didn't it?"

"Maddy, that's not the way it happened."

She raised an eyebrow. "Yes, it is, and I was too naive to catch on. I have 'gullible' tattooed on my forehead," she muttered. "That's why I'm picked up by strangers in train stations and how I get myself into these messes." She walked over to the bar and set her empty glass on the bar. "Well, cowboy, I've learned my lesson one more time. I won't be used by you or anyone else." She looked up at him, willing him to stop her, to say anything to make her believe that he really loved her.

He didn't say a word.

"I wish you luck tomorrow. Jenna needs to stay here with you. Anyone can see that, and I hope they do. If you'll excuse me, I'm going to bed."

"What are you going to do?" he asked, his voice hoarse.

She didn't look back. "I'm on vacation," she replied. "So I'm going to ride off into the sunset, of course."

IT WAS MORE LIKE RIDE off into the sunrise, Maddy realized. There was nowhere she could go at eleven o'clock at night, so she spent her last night tossing and turning and refusing to shed tears for her own gullible behavior.

He'd never said he loved her. Not once. She should have seen that as a major problem, but no. She'd only wanted to see the love in his eyes and feel the touch of his hands and his heart pounding against her skin. She'd wanted to believe he was in love with her, so she'd been a fool.

In the morning Maddy tiptoed into the kitchen and made a pot of coffee. Fortunately Stuart stayed out of the way, at least until Maddy poured herself a cup and retreated to her room to pack. Jenna knocked on the bedroom door and Maddy helped her hook the neckline of her dress.

The child threw herself into Maddy's arms, and Maddy held back tears. "Good luck," she whispered into the subdued blond curls. "Don't forget to stand up for yourself and what you want."

Jenna pulled back and sniffed. "I promise."

Maddy waited for the truck to drive away before she searched for Mac.

IF THERE WAS EVER a day he didn't want to live through again, this was it. Stuart pushed open the front door and Jenna ran past him toward the kitchen.

"Maddy," she called. "Maddy?"

It didn't surprise him that she'd left. He'd seen the look in her eyes before she'd turned away from him and said she was going to leave. She thought he'd been using her. Hell, that was the last thing he'd been doing, but Maddy hadn't believed that.

He followed Jenna into the kitchen and got a beer from the refrigerator as his daughter ran out of Maddy's bedroom.

"She's gone," the child yelled. *"Gone!"*

"I know. I figured she would be."

Jenna glared at him. "But she didn't want to go! She liked it here!"

"Not enough to stay," he muttered, watching Jenna throw herself into a chair. He thought it was time to change the subject before he threw the bottle through a window. "I was proud of you today."

Jenna didn't look up. "I just told the truth."

Thank God she had. He could still see her in that enormous leather chair in the judge's chambers. She'd ignored everyone around her and looked the judge in the eye and told him she wanted to stay with her father on the Triple J. The judge, a slender woman with a head of silver hair, asked several questions and listened carefully to Jenna's answers.

The lawyers had their say, and although Irene was on her best behavior, the judge expressed concern about uprooting a child from the home she'd known for almost ten years, especially a home the child didn't want to leave.

Thirty minutes later the adoption petition had been signed, and Jenna was officially Jenna Anderson.

And Jenna Anderson was furious with her father. "It's all your fault," she told him. "You should have asked her to stay."

Stuart set his beer bottle on the counter and crossed his arms in front of his chest. "It's not that simple."

"Yes, it is," she argued. "You could have made Mom stay that day, but you didn't."

Stuart straightened. "The day of the accident?"

"I heard you fighting. When she left, you just let her go." Tears began to run down Jenna's face. "Why didn't you try to stop her? She might not be dead if you'd stopped her!"

Stuart fought the sudden lump in his throat as he hurried to take his daughter in his arms. "I couldn't stop her, honey. I knew it wouldn't do any good," he said gently. "Your mother stopped listening to me a long time before that day." His arms tightened around her as she continued to cry. "If I could go back to that day, I'd do anything in my power to keep her from walking out that door. But I can't go back."

"You let Maddy leave."

He felt a sharp pain run through him. "That's not the same thing."

Jenna pulled away to glare at him. "Yes, it is. You could have stopped her, you could have made her stay here with us, but you didn't. You just let her go."

Stuart couldn't answer. There wasn't anything to say. The child was right. He could have stopped Maddy somehow, even if he'd had to tie her to a fence post to get her to listen to him. Instead, he'd hidden his feelings and let her walk out thinking he didn't love her, that he'd used her to try to win custody of Jenna.

"It's too late. I'm sorry."

"She can't have gone very far," Jenna argued. She took a napkin from the pile on the table and blew her nose. "Do you think she took the Lincoln?"

"We can go look, but I don't know if she'd come back if I found her," he admitted.

"Wait," Jenna ordered, and ran out of the room.

When she returned she had Maddy's old copy of *The Lights of the Desert Stars*. She handed it to her father. "This is her favorite book. There's gotta be something in here to tell you what she wants."

He took the book and stared down at the battered brown cover. "Maddy's idea of the Western cowboy," he muttered. "She was always suggesting I read it."

"Do it now," Jenna urged. "I'm gonna find Mac and see if he knows anything. Read fast, cuz she's getting farther away every minute!"

HE READ FOR FOUR HOURS without stopping except to stretch his legs a couple of times. Jenna brought him a peanut-butter-and-jelly sandwich for dinner. Mac came by to see if Maddy had called and if there was anything for dessert. She hadn't and there wasn't. Stuart read the ending twice and slapped the book shut. If Maddy wanted a cowboy, she was damn well going to get one. And once she got him, he wouldn't be so easy to get rid of, that was for sure.

DEMING'S BEST WESTERN motel wasn't far enough away, Maddy decided, but it was the best she could do for today. She'd checked the bus schedules and planned on taking the morning bus to Albuquerque and the airport there. There were no dude ranches in Madeleine Harmon's future; she was ready to go home. She was ready to turn her back on horses and cactus, cowboys and desert stars.

Madeleine refused to think of Stuart, knowing the ache in her heart would heal eventually. Those desert stars would soon shine down on the parking lot of the motel, but for her own peace of mind she'd pretend not to notice. She huddled in a chair and looked out the second-story window, waiting for her pizza delivery to arrive.

TACO, HIS FAVORITE horse, had never liked traffic but he was the only one Stuart could trust not to bolt. Riding down the main street of town, Stuart felt like the grand marshall in the damn Fourth of July parade. He wore his fanciest shirt, the one Mac had given him for a joke one Christmas, but he figured Maddy would appreciate it. He wished his jeans were a little newer, but he didn't have time to buy a pair. Jenna had polished his boots, though.

Quite a few kids waved at him, and a few fools even honked their horns. You'd think they'd never seen a man on a horse before.

He rode up in front of the registration office of the fourth motel he'd come to, and dismounted. It was almost sunset. If he didn't find Maddy soon, he'd have to load Taco onto the trailer and find a place to sleep tonight. Either that or hook a couple of flashlights on the saddle. He'd thought it would be easy to spot the Lincoln, but he wasn't sure where she'd leave it. She could have parked it anywhere and called Mac to tell him where to pick it up.

So his only choice was to stop at every motel in Deming until he found her. At least she'd told Mac that much when she left, for all the good it had done him.

"Madeleine Harmon?" The young man at the desk nodded as he looked up from the registration book. "Yep. She's here."

"I'm supposed to meet her here," Stuart explained, hoping the kid would feel intimidated enough to tell him anything he wanted. "What room is she in?" The young man hesitated, so Stuart attempted a smile.

"Don't mess with me, kid. I'm getting married in the morning."

"Two thirty-one." He gulped. "And congratulations."

"Thanks." Stuart turned away.

"Sir? What about the horse?"

"I'm taking him with me," he replied. He opened the door, making the bell jingle in response, and climbed back on Taco. He nudged the gelding into the parking lot. "Come on, fella. This is our big moment."

At first Maddy didn't recognize the cowboy astride the black horse trotting past the parked cars in the lot down below. Her first thought was that a rodeo rider was looking for an air-conditioned room for the night. Then the cowboy looked up at her and pulled his horse to a stop.

"Stuart?" She didn't know if she'd really said his name out loud or not, but he tipped his hat back and said something to the horse. She stood and hurried outside to the balcony. "Stuart?" she tried again. "What are you doing?"

"I've come to take you home."

"I told you, I'm not a housekeeper anymore."

"I don't want a housekeeper," he growled. "I want *you*."

The people in the pool stopped swimming and came closer to the fence to see what was going on. Maddy heard doors open downstairs and a child's voice called, "Look at the horsie, Mama!"

"You're attracting attention," she moaned. "Just go back to the ranch."

He ignored the eyes watching them and sat on the horse as if he had all the time in the world. "Don't you want to know what happened today?" When she didn't answer he continued on. "We won."

"I'm glad, really. But that doesn't have anything to do with me, except you don't need me anymore. Don't you see?"

"I read the book, Maddy."

"You did?"

He nodded. "Can't you tell? In the last chapter the cowboy goes after the woman he loves and rescues her from the Mexican bandits. What do you want me to rescue you from, Maddy?"

"I don't—"

"Let him rescue you, lady," one of the maids called. "Before that horse makes a mess in the parking lot."

"I taught you how to rope and ride and fish," he stated. "And other things. I kept all my promises, didn't I?"

Yes, she realized. He'd kept his promises.

"I want you, Maddy. And I need you, too," he called. "You were right, but I'm not going to apologize for that. I need you and you need me, too. But I should have told you I loved you, shouldn't I?"

Maddy stared down at him, wondering how she could possibly believe him. How she could *not* believe him. "Yes, you should have. Why don't you get off your horse and prove it?"

The crowd began to chuckle as Stuart dismounted, never taking his gaze from Maddy's face. He handed the reins to the chambermaid and took the metal stairs two at a time until he reached Maddy's side.

"You can write the last chapter this time, Maddy," he whispered, taking her into his arms. He kissed her for a long moment, as if he never wanted to let her go. Then he looked past her, toward the Western sky. "We could ride off into the sunset. We'll spend our honeymoon looking for the lost gold mine. Is that a good enough ending for you?"

Drawing him close again, she kissed him, realizing she'd found the cowboy she couldn't live without. "Yes," she murmured, as the crowd burst into applause. "It's perfect."

It's hot...
and it's out of control!

It's a two-alarm Blaze—
from one of Temptation's newest authors!

This spring, Temptation turns up the heat. Look
for these bold, provocative, *ultra*-sexy books!

#679 PRIVATE PLEASURES
Janelle Denison
April 1998

Mariah Stevens wanted a husband. Grey Nichols
wanted a lover. But Mariah was determined.
For better or worse, there would be no more private
pleasures for Grey without a public ceremony.

#682 PRIVATE FANTASIES
Janelle Denison
May 1998

For Jade Stevens, Kyle was the man of her dreams. He
seemed to know her every desire—in bed and out. Little
did she know that he'd come across her book of private
fantasies—or that he intended to make every one come true!

BLAZE! Red-hot reads from Temptation!

THE MEN OF BACHELOR CREEK

Alaska. A place where men could be men—and women were scarce!

To Tanner, Joe and Hawk, Alaska was the final frontier. They'd gone to the ends of the earth to flee the one thing they all feared—MATRIMONY. Little did they know that three intrepid heroines would brave the wilds to "save" them from their lonely bachelor existences.

Enjoy

**#662 CAUGHT UNDER
THE MISTLETOE!**
December 1997

#670 DODGING CUPID'S ARROW!
February 1998

#678 STRUCK BY SPRING FEVER!
April 1998

by Kate Hoffmann

Available wherever Harlequin books are sold.

Welcome to *Love Inspired*™

A brand-new series of contemporary inspirational love stories.

Join men and women as they learn valuable lessons about facing the challenges of today's world and about life, love and faith.

Look for the following April 1998 Love Inspired™ titles:

DECIDEDLY MARRIED
by Carole Gift Page

A HOPEFUL HEART
by Lois Richer

HOMECOMING
by Carolyne Aarsen

Available in retail outlets in March 1998.

LIFT YOUR SPIRITS AND GLADDEN YOUR HEART
with *Love Inspired!*™

Steeple Hill™

LI498

DEBBIE MACOMBER

invites you to the

HEART OF TEXAS

Join Debbie Macomber as she brings you the lives
and loves of the folks in the ranching community
of Promise, Texas.

If you loved Midnight Sons—don't miss
Heart of Texas! A brand-new six-book series
from Debbie Macomber.

Available in February 1998
at your favorite retail store.

Heart of Texas by Debbie Macomber

Lonesome Cowboy	February '98
Texas Two-Step	March '98
Caroline's Child	April '98
Dr. Texas	May '98
Nell's Cowboy	June '98
Lone Star Baby	July '98

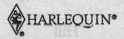

HARLEQUIN®

FIVE STARS MEAN SUCCESS

If you see the "5 Star Club" flash on a book, it means we're introducing you to one of our most STELLAR authors!

Every one of our Harlequin and Silhouette authors who has sold over 5 MILLION BOOKS has been selected for our "5 Star Club."

We've created the club so you won't miss any of our bestsellers. So, each month we'll be highlighting every original book within Harlequin and Silhouette written by our bestselling authors.

NOW THERE'S NO WAY ON EARTH OUR STARS WON'T BE SEEN!

OVER 5 MILLION BOOKS SOLD
SPECIAL OFFER INSIDE

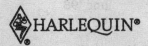 HARLEQUIN®

 Silhouette

LOVE & LAUGHTER™

Marriage Makers

by

Cathie Linz

Once upon a time, three bumbling fairy god-mothers set out to find the Knight triplets their soul mates. But... Jason was too sexy, Ryan was too stubborn and Anastasia was just too smart to settle down.

*But with the perfect match and a little fairy dust...
Happily Ever After is just a wish away!*

March 1998—
TOO SEXY FOR MARRIAGE (#39)

June 1998—
TOO STUBBORN TO MARRY (#45)

September 1998—
TOO SMART FOR MARRIAGE (#51)

Available wherever Harlequin books are sold.

WE KNOW YOU LIKED THIS ONE

Kristine Rolofson is a fabulous author whose books are highly acclaimed by romance fans everywhere. Reviewing *Madeleine's Cowboy*, *Romantic Times* praises Rolofson for delivering "a heartwarming love story." We're sure that you agree with the experts!

WE'RE POSITIVE YOU'LL LOVE THE NEXT BOOK FROM

⬧HARLEQUIN®
Temptation

Our stars will only keep rising! Kristine's next title will be just as good as her last—if not better. To make sure you don't miss it we're offering $1.00 off her next book or any Harlequin Temptation book.

**Look for *The Wrong Man in Wyoming*,
Harlequin Temptation #692, available in July 1998
at your favorite retail outlet.**

PBSAIS-HTUS